THE
JOURNEY
OF
IBN
FATTOUMA

Naguib Mahfouz ↝

THE JOURNEY OF IBN FATTOUMA

Translated by
Denys Johnson-Davies

DOUBLEDAY
New York London Toronto Sydney Auckland

PUBLISHED BY DOUBLEDAY
a division of Bantam Doubleday Dell Publishing Group, Inc.
666 Fifth Avenue, New York, New York 10103

DOUBLEDAY and the portrayal of an anchor with
a dolphin are trademarks of Doubleday,
a division of Bantam Doubleday Dell
Publishing Group, Inc.

The English translation of *The Journey of Ibn Fattouma* was first
published by The American University in Cairo Press in 1992.
First published in Arabic in 1983 as *Rihlat ibn Fattuma*.
Protected under the Berne Convention.
The Doubleday edition is published by arrangement with
The American University in Cairo Press.

Library of Congress Cataloging-in-Publication Data

Maḥfūẓ, Najīb, 1911–
    [Riḥlat Ibn Faṭṭūmah. English]
    The journey of Ibn Fattouma / Naguib Mahfouz ; translated by
Denys Johnson-Davies.
        p. cm.
    Translation of: Riḥlat Ibn Faṭṭūmah.
    I. Title.
PJ7846.A46R513   1992
892'.736—dc20   91-32886
                                                              CIP

ISBN 0-385-42323-3
Copyright © 1983 by Naguib Mahfouz
English translation copyright © 1992 by The American University in Cairo Press
ALL RIGHTS RESERVED
PRINTED IN THE UNITED STATES OF AMERICA
SEPTEMBER 1992
FIRST DOUBLEDAY EDITION

Contents

THE
JOURNEY
OF
IBN
FATTOUMA

I

The Homeland

Life and death, dreaming and wakefulness: stations for the perplexed soul. It traverses them stage by stage, taking signs and hints from things, groping about in the sea of darkness, clinging stubbornly to a hope that smilingly and mysteriously renews itself. Traveler, what are you searching for? What emotions rage in your heart? How will you govern your natural impulses and capricious thoughts? Why do you guffaw with laughter like a cavalier? Why do you shed tears like a child? You witness the pleasures of terpsichorean feasts, you see the executioner's sword as it lops off heads, and every action, fine or base, is initiated in the name of God the Merciful, the Compassionate. You are taken over in your ecstasy by protective shades as skilled as any sorcerer—the mother, the teacher, the loved one, and the chamberlain—protective shades that do not withstand the winds of Time but whose names remain crowned with immortality. However much the place distances itself from me it will continue to let fall drops of affection, conferring memories that are never forgotten, and etching its mark, in the name of the homeland, in the very core of the heart. So long as I live I shall passionately love the effusions of the perfume vendors; the minarets and the domes; the radiant face of a pretty girl illuminating the lane; the mules of the privileged and the feet of the barefooted; the songs of the deranged and the melodies of the rebab; the prancing steeds and the lablab trees; the cooing of pigeons and the plaintive call of doves.

My mother addresses me. "The day you were born."

She shakes her beautifully fashioned head and I say joyfully, "It was really *your* day."

My father was Muhammad al-Innabi, a prosperous grain merchant. He produced seven notable merchant sons and lived till he was over eighty, enjoying good health and vigor. At the age of eighty he saw my beautiful mother, Fattouma al-Azhari, who was then a young girl of seventeen, the last child born to a butcher called al-Azhari Qatayef. She took my father's heart by storm. He married her and lived with her in a spacious house he bought in her name, occasioning much fury and uproar in his family. My brothers regarded the marriage as a squalid and illicit piece of fun, and they sought the intervention of the cadi and the head of the merchants, but my father slipped from their grasp. He was like a lover stripped of all willpower. He deemed marriage a right that was not open to discussion and the difference in age an illusion used as an argument by those who were biased. He went on drinking from the source of his happiness with a heart full of confidence.

"And your birth brought both confirmation of their defeat and renewal of their fury."

And often I would say to her, "There is no limit to man's greed!"

From my early youth I would be addressed with the pleasantest of words but cruelly exposed to the ugliest of treatment. My father called me Qindil, but my brothers gave me the name Ibn Fattouma, Son of Fattouma, washing their hands of any possible relationship with them and casting doubts upon my mother.

My father died before his image became engraved on my consciousness, leaving us with enough money to assure us of an agreeable life until the end of our days. The quarrel between us and my brothers was interrupted, but my mother feared for us both and became so carried away by misgivings and doubts that she decided not to send me to the elementary school. She put me instead in the charge of Sheikh Maghagha al-Gibeili, a neighbor of her family, to instruct me at home. From him I received lessons in the Quran, the Sayings of the Prophet, philology, arithmetic, belles-lettres, jurisprudence, Sufism, and the literature of travels. A man in his forties, he was strong and of dignified appearance, with an elegant beard, tall turban, and comely jubba; he had bright, penetrating eyes and would deliver the lesson in a full voice which he used in a quietly deliberate manner, subduing all difficulties by the excellence of his explanations and the gentleness of his smile. My mother, benefiting from a lengthy period of leisure, would follow the lessons attentively from behind a screen when we were in the hall in winter, and through an aperture when we were in the reception room during the other seasons.

"I see you're happy with your teacher," she would say to me. "That's very fortunate."

"He's a great sheikh," I would tell her enthusiastically.

He used to allot a certain time to discussion, when he would put forward such questions as occurred to him and would invite me to make known my own thoughts, treating me like a grown-up.

Then one day—I don't remember how old I was—I asked him, "If Islam is as you say it is, why are the streets packed with poor and ignorant people?"

"Islam today," he answered me sorrowfully, "skulks in the mosques and doesn't go beyond them to the outside world."

He would speak at length, castigating the prevailing conditions. Even the Sultan was not immune from his criticism.

"Then it is Satan who is controlling us, not the Revelation," I said.

"I congratulate you on your words," he said approvingly. "They are greater than your years."

"And what is to be done, Master?"

"You are intelligent," he said calmly. "Be patient."

As for what he had to say about travels, it instilled in me both passion and joy. During his discourse he talked about a certain ancient traveler.

"I myself," he continued, "came to know traveling in the company of my late father, and we roamed the East and the West."

"Tell me about the things you saw, Master," I said eagerly.

He spoke so liberally that I lived in my imagination the vast lands of the Muslims, and my own homeland seemed to me like a star in a sky crammed with stars.

"But you will not come across anything really new in the lands of Islam," he said.

My eyes inquired of him the reason and he said, "All of them are close in circumstance, inclination, and ritual, all of them far distant from the spirit of true Islam. But you will discover new and strange lands in the southern desert. . . ."

He aroused my yearnings to the bursting point. Then he said, "I undertook that journey on my own, following the death of my father. I visited the lands of Mashriq, Haira, and Halba, and had it not been for unfavorable circumstances I would have visited Aman, Ghuroub, and Gebel, but the caravan came to a stop at Halba because civil war was breaking out in Aman.

"And they are heathen lands," he said, fixing me with a strange look.

"God forbid!" I exclaimed.

"But both there and on the way the stranger will find nothing but security, owing to the pressing need for trade and travelers."

"But it's abominable!"

"The observer is under no compulsion," he said quietly.

"And why didn't you repeat the experience?"

"The circumstances of life and family made me forget the most important objective of the journey, which was to visit the land of Gebel."

"And what's the importance of the land of Gebel?" I asked him eagerly.

"You hear a lot about it," he said with a sigh. "It's as though it were the miracle of countries, as though it were perfection itself, incomparable perfection."

"Many travelers have doubtless written about it."

"I have never in my life," he said in a tone not devoid of sorrow, "met a human being who has paid it a visit, nor have I found a book or manuscript about it."

"It's an extraordinary, unbelievable thing," I said, dejected.

"It's a closed secret," he said gloomily.

And like any closed secret it drew me to its edge and plunged me into its darkness. My imagination was fired.

Whenever I was upset by a word or action, my soul fluttered around the land of Gebel.

Sheikh Maghagha al-Gibeili continued to enlighten my mind and spirit, dispersing the darkness from around me and directing my cravings to that which is most noble in life. My mother was happy at what I was gaining day by day and participated in shaping me by her love and her beauty. She was of medium height and slender build; her complexion was fair and exuded a sweet serenity. Never did she hesitate to express her admiration for my handsomeness, though telling me with the same frankness, "Your words often disturb my peace of mind."

I inquired the reason and she said, "It's as though you see only the ugly side of life."

She would not deny what I said or see therein any exaggeration, but she expressed her faith with the words "God is the Maker of everything and He has in everything an underlying reason."

"I am upset by injustice, poverty, and ignorance."

"God demands that we be content in all circumstances," she insisted.

I raised the subject for discussion with the sheikh, but his attitude was perfectly clear, believing as he did in the intellect and in freedom of choice, though he gently whispered in my ear, "Avoid distressing your mother."

It was advice that I was bound to follow, driven and supported as I was by my great love for her. I found no difficulty in that, for her guilelessness was on a par with her beauty. However, the days that brought me lessons and instruction also pushed me to the threshold of adolescence, so that the skies poured down fresh rains and places of interest manifested themselves in the light of fresh torch flares.

"What are you intending to do in this life whose only fulfillment is through work?" Sheikh Maghagha al-Gibeili asked me.

But I was seeing Halima Adli al-Tantawi in a new way. For a long time I had seen her, during my years of boyhood, leading her father, the blind Quran reciter. They had a small, old house in the alley in which our own stood shining like a star. My attention would pass her by and attach itself to her father with his thin frame, his blanked-out eyes and coarse, pockmarked nose. He aroused my sympathy and my astonishment, while I admired his voice as he gave the call to prayer, rendering this voluntary service in front of the door of his house. The quickly passing days turned my attention to the girl and I discovered her anew. The ground of the alley was slippery as a result of a light shower, and the old man was walking cautiously, having given his left arm to his daughter and his right to a thick stick that felt out positions for his feet with successive taps like a chicken's beak searching for grain. Halima walked alongside him wholly enveloped in a dark, flowing garment from which there showed, from the lowered veil, nothing but two eyes. But her form took on, to my eyes impregnated with the freshness of recent manhood, the shape of a consummate female, her shielded jewels coming to life whenever the breeze blew against her garment, as though they were burning coals under ashes. Her foot slipped, or almost did, and she braced herself quickly so as to retain her balance, at which her head made an involuntary movement that caused the veil to drop from her face. Thus it became wholly imprinted on my sight, its beauty embedded in the nooks and crannies of my very being. In a fleeting moment I received a long message charged with all the intimations that determine the fate of a heart.

My mother, on the strength of Sheikh Maghagha's words about work fulfilling one's life, asked me, "Do you not agree that commerce would suit you best?"

I astonished her by saying, "I am thinking first of all of marriage."

She warmly welcomed the postponement of discussion about work, and she started describing to me certain daughters of merchants. Once again, though, I astonished her by saying, "My choice has fallen on Halima the daughter of Sheikh Adli al-Tantawi."

My mother did not conceal the shock she felt. "In everything she is below what is demanded."

"But I want her," I insisted.

"Your brothers will gloat over us because of your unfortunate choice."

But my brothers were like something that had never been, as my feeling that I was the man of the house was growing with time. She did not oppose me, though she gave her agreement grudgingly, while at the same time not losing hope.

All of a sudden things went in accordance with my wishes, even though at a heavy price. My mother's opposition had lessened until she said to me resignedly, "Your happiness is dearer to me than any other consideration." At once she undertook what was expected of her and went from our mansion to the shabby house and asked for Halima's hand for me. On a later occasion she took me with her and we sat with Sheikh Adli al-Tantawi and his wife, and the bride made her appearance and revealed such parts of the face and hands as the religious law permits, stayed for a few minutes and left. The preparations for the wedding were made with commendable speed.

Then one day I noticed that my teacher, Sheikh Maghagha al-Gibeili, was suffering from a certain unusual embarrassment and that he was talking to me in a quite new tone. Looking down at his slippers, he said quietly, "There is an important matter, Qindil."

My curiosity was much aroused. "I'm at your disposal," I said.

"I can no longer bear my solitude," he said sadly.

The sheikh was a widower. He had three daughters who had married and were settled in their homes.

"And why do you remain alone?" I asked him innocently. "Did not the Prophet, may the blessings and peace of God be upon him, marry following the death of his wife Khadija?"

"You're right, and that's what I'm thinking of doing."

"You are a man," I said warmly, "who would be welcome in the noblest of families."

"But my request is in none other than your own family," he said shyly.

"My family?"

"Yes," he said humbly. "Your lady mother."

"But my mother won't marry," I said hurriedly.

"Why not, Qindil?"

Briefly at a loss, I said, "She's my mother."

"Marriage," he said quietly, "is the law of the Almighty. It won't be easy for you to marry and to leave your mother on her own." He was silent for a while, then said, "May God guide us to the right path."

In my loneliness, my thoughts clashed together and events arranged themselves in my mind in a new and gloomy form. I told myself that my mother's sudden

compliance with my wish to marry Hailma had re-
sulted only from her own wish to be married to Sheikh
Maghagha al-Gibeili. Innocent things had happened behind my back, yet they stuck in my gullet. I found myself
in a delicate position between, on the one hand, the two
persons most dear to me in life and, on the other, my
anger, indignation, and embarrassment.

"O Lord," I exclaimed from the depths of my soul,
"save me from wrong and stupidity."

The truth is that I behaved in a way worthier of a
person older in both years and experience. I let matters
proceed in accordance with God's will and persuaded my
mutinous self that marriage was the right of man and
woman; that my mother was not only a mother but also
a woman; and that we had been created in order that we
might endure the truth and stand up to it, receiving our
share of pleasure and pain with the courage of believers.
I took upon my shoulders the experience in all its dimen-
sions and spoke to my mother of the matter with my
customary frankness. She exhibited an astonishment that
irritated me.

"It didn't occur to me," she muttered.

"But it's only right and just," I said coolly.

I went on digesting my sense of frustration as she said
falteringly, "I want a chance to think it over."

I regarded that as the first sign of agreement, so inconsistent was it with the manner of open refusal, and I

waited with dispirited heart till she whispered to me with bashful confusion, "Let it be as God wills."

I pondered about how we embellish our longings with luminous words of piety, and how we conceal our shyness with firebrands of divine inspiration.

The usual preparations were made for the marriage of both son and mother, and it was agreed that my mother should transfer to the house of Sheikh Maghagha, a pleasant enough house, and that Halima should come to the mansion. I determined to take refuge in the happiness that had been afforded me and to shake off the residue of my worries. However, destiny descended upon us and scattered our plans to the winds. The Sultan's third chamberlain shoved his way into our quiet life and, like a tempest, took it by storm. One day, having seen Halima, he decided to have her as his fourth wife. Sheikh Adli al-Tantawi, in terror, said to my teacher, Sheikh Maghagha, "I am incapable of refusing."

Trembling, he rescinded our engagement and Halima was given in marriage, between one day and the next, to the third chamberlain. In a stupor I withdrew within myself, wondering about Halima's heart, about her innermost feelings. Did she share my pain or was she intoxicated and dazzled by the glitter of wealth? In my loneliness I found myself saying, "I have been betrayed by religion, betrayed by my mother, betrayed by Halima. God's curse be upon this adulterated land!"

Everything looked gloomy. From the simplest of individuals like Sheikh Adli al-Tantawi right up to the Sultan himself, and including every kind of person and behavior, all deserved the Flood, so that a new and clean world might replace them. I was not touched by my mother's sympathy and sadness or by the maxims Sheikh Maghagha sprinkled upon me. The world appeared loathsomely jaundiced, not to be borne or lived in.

"You should marry as soon as possible," my mother told me. "Perhaps God is keeping in store for you something better than you yourself chose."

I shook my head in rejection.

"Begin to work without delay," said Sheikh Maghagha.

Again I shook my head, to which the man said, "No doubt you have a plan?"

"To undertake a journey," I said, giving expression to the emotions that flooded me.

"What journey?" inquired my mother in alarm. "You're hardly twenty years of age."

"It's the most suitable age for traveling," I said. Looking at my teacher for a while, I went on, "I shall visit Mashriq, Haira, and Halba, but I shall not stop, as you did because of the civil war that had broken out in Aman—I shall visit Aman and Ghuroub and Gebel. How long would I require for that?"

"You would require at least a year, if not more," said

Sheikh Maghagha al-Gibeili, regarding my mother with concern.

"That's not too much for someone seeking wisdom," I said resolutely. "I want to learn and to return to my ailing homeland with a remedy to heal her."

My mother was about to speak, but I forestalled her by saying firmly, "It's a decision I shall not go back on."

The dream gained mastery of me and my sense of reality vanished. The land of Gebel presented itself to the eye of my imagination like some much-loved star mounting its throne behind the other stars. The eternal desire for travel ripened in the flame of continued pain. Sheikh Maghagha al-Gibeili, yielding to the inevitable, invited the owner of the caravan to take dinner with us. He was a man in his forties by the name of al-Qani ibn Hamdis, and he was strong of build and judgment.

"I would like him to go with you and to return with you," said Sheikh Maghagha.

"That depends upon his wish. We stay in each land ten days, so he who is content with that proceeds on with us, and he who wants to stay longer remains behind. In any event there is a caravan every ten days."

"Ten days anywhere is long enough," said Sheikh Maghagha to me.

"I think so," I said.

As for my mother, she concentrated on the question of safety.

"A caravan," said the man simply, "is never subjected to attack. The inhabitants themselves enjoy a mere hundredth of the protection afforded to strangers."

I began making preparations for the journey, whilst seeking guidance from my teacher, Sheikh Maghagha. Thus I filled one case with dinars, a second with clothes, and a third with odds and ends including notebooks, pens, and books. I thought it best that my mother's marriage to the sheikh should take place before I set out. However, the sheikh moved to the mansion so that it should not be left empty. I attained a new mood and thought less about my sorrows. The journey dominated my senses, and an unlimited scope for hope was opened up before me.

2
The Land of Mashriq

My mother bade me a warm and tearful farewell, saying, "Would that God had spared us all this, but it was your wish."

"In any event, I have not left you on your own," I said to myself, and Sheikh Maghagha al-Gibeili accompanied me to the excise tax square, which we reached just before dawn and where we saw the caravan by the light of torches. The darkness spread all around us, breathing in the breezes of spring, while above us the vigilant stars exchanged glances. Sheikh Maghagha whispered in my ear, "Don't fail to catch Ibn Hamdis' caravan."

At the same time the voice of the owner of the caravan was raised as he called, "Departure is right after the dawn prayers."

"All your companions are merchants," he said to me as we shook hands, "and you are the only traveler amongst us."

That neither pleased nor displeased me. The call to prayer hovered above our heads, so we made our way towards the market mosque and arranged ourselves in ranks for the last community prayers we would have the chance of performing. We hurried out of the mosque to the caravan and took our places with the traveling bags. The column of camels began to move off to the rhythm of the singing of the cameleer and my heart became immersed in the tender pain of saying farewell. Deep within me there stirred memories of my mother and of Halima, wrapped around in a grief that encompassed my whole motherland. In the heart of the darkness I mumbled, "O God, bless the steps I take."

The darkness began to clear and streaks of light loomed on the horizon until it became tinged with a smiling redness, and the eyebrow of the sun emerged, unrolling light over a limitless desert. The caravan showed itself like a dancing line on a cosmic surface challenging sublimity. My body plunged into a successively monotonous movement under waves of gushing light, a gliding breeze, a heat that rose upwards giving warning of its ferocity, and a constant landscape of yellow sands and a clear blue sky. I took refuge within myself from the single panorama and sank into insistent memories, bitter emotions, and rosy dreams. At every spring of water we would make a stop for food, ablutions, prayers, and conversation. I got to know a few of the merchants accompanying me, who cast strange glances upon the sole traveler.

"I shall go right to the land of Gebel," I explained boastfully.

"And what is Gebel?" one of them inquired scornfully.

A second man said proudly, "We're in the lands of Islam."

A third said, "Trading is part of being civilized and God has ordered that we should be civilized."

A fourth said, "The Prophet, may the blessings and peace of God be upon him, was a merchant."

"And he was also a traveler and a man who emigrated from his place of birth," I said, as though making excuses for myself.

"You'll fritter away your fortune in traveling and will return home poor."

"He who believes in work will not know poverty," I said, suppressing my anger.

I had a respect for trading, but I believed that life was as much a journey as it was commerce. The days followed one another, long and heavy, hot during the day, cold at night. I saw the stars as I had never seen them before, sublime, enchanting, infinite, and I knew that my sadness for my mother was greater than I had imagined and that my love for Halima was too strong to be influenced by the night and the day and the stars and looking towards the unknown. We had been going for nearly a month when from afar the walls of Mashriq came into view, at which al-Qani ibn Hamdis said, "We shall camp at the Blue Well and shall enter the land at midnight."

We prepared ourselves, and when we had prayed the

evening prayer, I heard someone whisper, "The last prayer until we return from the lands of idolatry."

I was extremely disturbed, but I was preparing myself for a new and long life, so I said to myself, "God is forgiving and merciful."

Just before midnight the caravan approached the new land. We were met at the entrance by a man naked but for a loincloth. In the light of the torch flares he appeared tall and thin; my companions said he was the director of customs. The man spoke in a stentorian voice. "Welcome to Mashriq, capital of the land of Mashriq. It greets traders and travelers, and he who keeps himself to himself will meet only with what is good and beautiful."

The caravan entered between two ranks of guards. The traders continued on to the market, while a guide took me to the inn of the foreigners. The guide made the camel kneel down in front of a large pavilion like a barracks. When he carried my traveling bags inside, I realized that it was the inn. It was divided into two wings separated by an extended reception hall; each wing contained adjoining rooms whose sides were constructed of hair cloth. The room chosen for me was simple, even primitive; its floor was sandy, and it possessed a bed (which consisted of a wooden board laid on the ground), a chest for clothes, and cushions in the middle. No sooner had I finished checking through my bags than I hurried to bed with the eagerness of someone deprived of normal sleep for a full month. I slept deeply until woken by the day's heat. As though unwell, I rose from my bed and passed through into the reception hall, which was crammed with guests, all of whom were seated in front of their rooms having breakfast. A short man, slightly stout, wearing only a loincloth, came up to me. "I am Fam, the owner of the inn," he said, smiling. "Did you have a good night?"

"Fine, thank you," I said, with the sweat pouring down my forehead.

"Shall I bring you breakfast?"

"I'd really like to have a wash," I said with longing.

He led me to the end of the reception hall, and drew back a curtain, where I found what I needed for washing and for combing my hair and small beard. Returning to my room, I found that Fam had brought a small round table and was laying out breakfast for me.

"Can I make my prayers in my room?" I asked.

"Someone might see you," he warned, "and you would run the risk of trouble."

He brought me a dish with some dried dates, milk, and barley bread. I ate with pleasure till I had satisfied my hunger.

"I used to love traveling," he told me.

"Are you from Mashriq?" I asked.

"I'm originally from the desert. Then I took up residence in Mashriq."

I was delighted to find he was a former traveler.

"The land of Gebel is the ultimate goal of my journey," I said.

"It is the goal of many. But material considerations prevented me from reaching it."

"What do you know about it, Mr. Fam?" I inquired eagerly.

"Nothing," he said, smiling, "except that it is sometimes described as the miracle of the age. And yet I have never met a single man who has visited it."

An inner voice told me that I would be the first human being to be given the chance of touring the land of Gebel and of making known its secret to the world.

"Are you staying long in Mashriq?" he asked.

"Ten days. After that I shall proceed with the caravan of al-Qani ibn Hamdis."

"Excellent. Go, look, and enjoy your time. It's enough for you to wear a loincloth and nothing more."

"I can't go out without a cloak," I said disapprovingly.

"You'll see for yourself," he said, laughing. "I forgot to ask you your name."

"Qindil Muhammad al-Innabi."

He raised his hand to his head in salutation and went off. At noon I left the inn wrapped round in a light, loosely woven cloak and wearing my turban to protect myself from the sun. I was astonished at the heat of spring and wondered what the heat of summer would be like.

On leaving the inn I was appalled by two things: the nakedness and the empty space.

The people, women and men alike, were as naked as the day they were born. Nakedness there is a commonplace; it attracts no attention and arouses no interest. Everyone goes his own way, finding nothing strange about it, apart from foreigners like myself who are wearing clothes. Their bodies are bronze-colored and thin, not gracefully so but apparently from undernourishment, though they mostly looked contented, even cheerful. I found it difficult to avoid a sense of abnormality in the clothes I was strutting around in; I found even greater difficulty in turning away my gaze from exciting spectacles of nudity which fired my blood. "What land is this that hurls a young man like me into the flames of temptation!"

The other strange thing was this vast, empty space; it was as though I had moved from one desert to another. Was this in truth the capital city of Mashriq? Where were the palaces? The houses? The streets? The alleyways? Nothing but open ground, with grass growing along the edges, on which cattle grazed. Here and there were groupings of tents set up haphazardly; in front were gathered women and young girls, spinning or milking cows and goats. They too were naked; and though possessed of a certain beauty this was hidden by filth, neglect, and poverty. In fact I criticize too harshly the outward signs of misery in this pagan country, which, being pagan, did perhaps have some excuse. But what excuse could I make for similar signs in my own Islamic country? "Look, record, and admit the bitter truth."

While my eyes were roving round in surprise and perplexity, I was suddenly overwhelmed by a sensation of being passionately in love, a feeling drawn out of the depths by the lover hidden within me. The memory of Halima overpowered me and her image enveloped the vastness with the warmth of sunrays. For a time I was at a loss; but then I became aware of a young girl running from the direction of the inn, and moving like an arrow towards a dense crowd, where she sank into the torrential mass and disappeared from sight. Perhaps I had spotted her previously; perhaps I had spotted her while I was occupied with the sights and she had made her impression when I was half asleep or in a daze. It was she who was behind the deep emotional agitation that swept over me. She was in truth Mashriqi, bronze and naked, but in her face she very closely resembled Halima, my lost love. I decided to be content with the thought that she was the Halima of Mashriq, and that I would see her again. I roamed about from place to place, seeing nothing new, enduring a lassitude that became more and more intense, with my heart crushed by grief and distress and my imagination searching for the Halima of Mashriq.

Away from home, I am remolded in a new form; in the depths of me there come into existence bold, impetuous longings to satisfy desires, to pursue adventures. I relinquish one civilization and give myself over to a new one. I yearn for life far away from observers: observers who, while manifesting themselves outwardly, also throb within oneself.

In the afternoon I found myself on the edge of a new empty space, not knowing how my tired feet had led me there; a clean, empty space devoid of cattle and herdsmen, bordered on both sides by tall, bulky trees, the like of which I had not seen before. Deep inside was a palace with a surrounding wall. The entrances to it were guarded by ranks of heavily armed horsemen. In the open square there was only a party of strangers like myself gazing in astonished admiration. How had this palace come to be put up among the tents? It was without doubt the palace of the king of Mashriq, and it was of course not permitted for one to visit it. I had thought that the ruler of Mashriq was nothing but a tribal chief living in a tent of suitable size and elegance.

"Is this the king's palace?" I asked one of the strangers.

"It would seem so," he answered with interest.

In truth it was no less grand than the palace of the Sultan in my homeland, though it looked strange and out of place in its surroundings.

The weather began to cool and to unveil its spring

face. But feelings of tiredness and hunger erupted like a ghoul, so I made my way back to the inn. I found Fam sitting on a bench of palm leaves at the entrance. He met me with a smile and asked, "Did you have your lunch in the market?"

"I haven't yet found where the market is," I said hastily, "and I'm dying of hunger, kind sir."

I sat down at the round table in front of my room and Fam brought me barley bread, a slice of beef fried in oil and vinegar, and a plate filled with dates, persimmons, and grapes.

"Shall I bring you some date wine?" he asked.

I was just going to set about the food with appetite. "God forbid," I said.

"Wine is the music of journeys," the man murmured.

I ate till I was satisfied, then asked if I might sit with him on the bench. He was very welcoming, so we sat with the evening slipping by under a moon not quite full. I received sweet breezes quite different from the boiling heat of the day, and soon a sense of peaceful languor crept over me.

"There are tents where there's music and dancing— just what the stranger would wish for," said Fam.

"Let's put that off for the time being," I said.

"Did you like what you saw?"

"The only thing worth seeing is the palace," I said

listlessly. "But I need information which one ordinarily doesn't get on the street."

"You're right."

"The king's palace is a real wonder."

"There's no king in the land of Mashriq," he said, smiling.

Perhaps he read the astonishment in my face, for he continued, "Mashriq consists of a capital and four towns. Each town has an overlord who is its owner; he owns the pastures, the cattle, and the herdsmen. The people are his slaves, they submit to his will in exchange for a sufficiency of subsistence and security. So the palace you saw is that of the overlord of the capital. He is the greatest and richest of the overlords, but he has no control over any of the others. Each overlord has his own armed force of mercenaries whom he usually brings from the desert."

What a strange system! It reminded me of the tribes in Arabia in the times before Islam, and yet it was different. It also reminded me of the landowners in my homeland, but again with a difference. They all represent different degrees of injustice. In any event, our own erring, in the land of Revelation, is more shocking than that of the rest of mankind. On my guard, I contented myself with listening and withheld my critical observations, as befits a stranger. "How was this splendid palace put up, when all the overlord's subjects are simple herdsmen?" I asked.

Fam answered with pride. "He brought engineers and workers from the land of Haira and acquired the most beautiful furnishings and works of art that the land of Halba can boast of."

I was silent for a while, then said, "Tell me, Fam, about your religion."

"All the people of Mashriq worship the moon. At the full moon the god appears in his perfection, so they hurry out to the open space and form a circle round the priest for prayers, then they practice his rites by dancing, singing, drinking, and making love."

I was greatly amazed. "And thus they assure themselves eternity in heaven?"

"We know neither eternity nor heaven—all we have is the night of the full moon."

"Is there no medicine and education?" I asked after a slight pause.

"The sons of the overlord learn horsemanship and information about the moon god. In every palace there is a doctor who comes from Haira or Halba. As for the ordinary people, they are left to nature, and anyone who falls ill is isolated until he is cured or dies, when he is eaten by predatory birds." I glanced at him questioningly and he went on, "It is the law of the moon and its teachings, which are completely consistent with life. So it is that we are a people who are content and cheerful most of the time. We are the happiest of peoples, Mr. Qindil."

I told myself that this was a state of unconsciousness, neither more nor less. However, I said, "Congratulations, Mr. Fam."

I spent part of the night writing in my notebook the chronicle of my journey and the sights I had seen. Another part of the night was taken up lying awake and thinking about the circumstances and ideas I had met with. I pondered over the torments suffered by human beings in this life and wondered whether in fact there was to be found in the land of Gebel the elixir for all ills.

The days passed without event, except that I found the courage to dress more skimpily, making do with short trousers and a skullcap. Then, one morning, I came unexpectedly upon an unusual movement of people rushing about and a whispered exchange of words among the guests. I hurried off to Fam to ask him what it was about.

"This is the night of the full moon," he exclaimed. "The night of worship and the appearance of the god."

I was excited by the news. He promised me that whoever saw it would find it a truly happy spectacle. I at once made my way to the market, where I met my merchant companions, who were encamped at its entrance. They were spending their days working and their nights in the places of entertainment. They had quickly become engrossed, with expert endeavor, in the business of barter, though I noticed that they did not deal with the locals but only with the representatives of the overlord of the

capital, for he alone was both buyer and seller. As for the
rest of the market, it consisted of a passageway with tents
set up on both sides for the selling of foodstuffs and
simple articles like combs, small mirrors, and cheap bead
jewelry.

I took my lunch in the inn, and then, with the sun
inclining towards the west, went to the square of worship.
The people, men and women, were gathering, forming
themselves into a dense circle, with the center empty.
Naked, they waited, their bronze bodies exuding sweat
and discharging into the atmosphere an exciting animal
smell. Before the setting of the sun, clouds rushed past
and obscured the blue dome of the sky, and for five
minutes drizzle rained down and was greeted with shouts
of joy from mouths filled with faith and a readiness for
adventure. No sooner had the sun disappeared than the
full moon strode forward, rising up from the opposite
side of the sky, grand and majestic. The people shouted
with joy, putting the birds of the air to fright. The moon
continued to rise, dispersing its golden light over the
naked bodies, their arms outstretched as though to clutch
the swimming orb of light. A considerable passage of
time went by in awed silence until the moon came to rest
in the very center of the sky. At that there sounded from
somewhere a long warning note on a trumpet, and a path
was opened up in the north side of the circle, making
way for a venerable figure: tall of stature, with flowing,

disheveled beard, his body naked. He came forward supporting himself on a long stick until he stood at the center of the circle. All eyes were fixed on the moon priest, and the silence grew more intense. The man stayed motionless for a while, then he let the stick fall to his feet and raised his head and arms towards the moon, and thousands upon thousands of arms imitated him. He clapped his hands and there burst forth in a single moment from the people's throats a single hymn; it burst forth, strong and universal, as though the earth and the sky and everything between them had joined forces, intoxicated with the singing and the ardor of lovers. A tune full of passion made its way to the depths of my being, a tune distinguished by a barbaric crudeness, exalted by reverberating echoes that stirred my heart with emotions of awesome pleasure. It ascended to a peak of explosion, then began a slow descent, step by step, until it let itself be lulled into a sleep of stillness and silence. The priest lowered his arms and looked above him; arms followed his, eyes turned to him. With dignified bearing he picked up his stick and, grasping it in his left hand, he commenced speaking.

"Here is the god manifesting himself in his beauty and majesty, appearing at his appointed time, not abandoning his slaves. How wonderful is the god, how blessed are his slaves!" From the surrounding sea of people there rose a murmur of thanks. The priest continued, "In his rotation he tells us that life knows no permanence and that it is towards waning that it makes its way. Yet it is good to those who are good, smiling to those who smile, so do not squander its riches in folly." Shrill cries of joy burst forth from the throats of the crowd like shooting stars and hands clapped to a dancing rhythm. The priest went on, "Beware of dispute, beware of evil. Hatred rends the liver, greed causes indigestion to the stomach and brings about disease. Avidity is a calamitous affliction. Be joyful and play, conquer wicked thoughts with contentment."

Immediately the beating of drums was heard and bodies weaved as they danced. The call was answered by breasts and buttocks. The movement continued, spreading out and extending under the light of the moon. The earth danced and the full moon blessed it. Embraces mingled with the dancing, everyone merging into universal lovemaking under the moonlight. I looked on with stupefied gaze, as though in an adolescent dream, my blood boiling in my veins, my desires colliding together madly, my heart yearning for madness. I returned to the inn, staggering from the state of excitement I was in, with the grip of lust pulling violently at my inflamed nerves. I remained in my room, staying awake by the light of a candle, writing down words in my notebook and thinking of the trials that lay in wait for my faith and my piety, reminding myself of the time of my religious and intel-

lectual education at the hands of Sheikh Maghagha al-
Gibeili. I gave myself over to my thoughts in a miserable
state of languor until, all of a sudden, my ear was pierced
by a shout for help. I jumped to my feet in a state of
readiness and found myself in utter darkness. I quickly
grasped that I had been asleep, that in fact sleep was
covering the whole universe. I had awoken early.

"Can I as a foreigner meet the sage of the capital?" I
asked as I was about to leave the inn.

"He is the moon's priest," said Fam. "He is always
happy to meet foreigners. I'll arrange a meeting with
him."

I went to the market but did not find any of the merchants. Al-Qani ibn Hamdis informed me that they had
gone to the palace to complete certain formalities with
the chamberlain of the overlord.

"Have you decided to journey on with my caravan?"
he asked me.

"Yes," I answered automatically. "There's nothing else
here worth seeing."

"You're right, for it's a poor country, but the coming
journeys promise places of great interest."

"What really is important to me is the land of Gebel,"
I said earnestly.

"May God grant you enjoyment of the most beautiful
things He has created," he said, smiling.

The boredom and heat became trying, so I went off to

amuse myself by walking in the market. By chance I paused and stood in wonder before the tent of an old man selling dates in boxes of palm leaves. Behind him, deep within the tent, I had spotted the alluring girl, the Halima of Mashriq, bronze and naked, feeding a pigeon and moving about with her elegant body and that ripeness that had not yet been spoiled. I stood agape, forgetful of myself, seeing only the girl standing in front of my eyes, and remembering, through her, Halima with her face like the full moon, her black eyes, her long neck. I was seeing the whole of my heart's history brought together in the image of a moment: in its center there met the awakening of the past, the magic of the present, and the dream of the future. What passion poured into my soul from that unique conformation! What a summons and what a shackling! I stared at her, drowned in her, ignoring her old father, my innate shyness, and the restraints that good manners imposed upon me. I forgot completely the boredom and the heat, the projects and the dreams of the journey and of Gebel, even the accumulated hopes of being back in my homeland. I forgot everything because I possessed everything: contentment, delight, and riches were locked in my bosom. The girl withdrew, becoming hidden from my sight, and I found myself alone with the fixed gaze of the old man. With my happy madness abated, I fell again into the grip of daily life with its temptations and sweat, and I proceeded to move away. I became aware of the voice of an old man calling.

"Stranger!"

I told myself I was guilty of something I should have been on my guard against. I turned round and stopped.

"Come here," he said gently.

I approached shyly and he asked, "Doesn't my daughter Arousa please you?"

I was tongue-tied with astonishment and made no answer.

"Doesn't Arousa please you?" he asked again. "There's no one like her in Mashriq."

"Please excuse me," I muttered in confusion.

"No young man has seen her without falling in love with her," he boasted.

"I never meant any harm," I said in apology, thinking that he was making fun of me.

"I don't understand the language of foreigners. Answer me: Does she please you?"

I hesitated a while, then said, "She's worthy of every admiration."

"Answer me frankly: Does she please you?"

I lowered my head in admission.

"Come in," he said.

I hesitated and he took me by the hand and drew me inside. He called Arousa and she came forward in all her

Naguib Mahfouz

nudity and stared at me until he asked, "What do you think of this foreigner who is in love with you?"

Without shyness or faltering she answered, "He's acceptable, Father."

"At last the moon has shed light on you!"

He took us to a corner of the tent and lowered a curtain. I found myself alone with her, and apparently secure, but I was in such confusion that it spoiled for me the utter happiness that was presented. Did this mean marriage in this land? Did it mean the abandonment I had witnessed being practiced under the light of the moon? She continued to look at me and to wait, while my love rushed out to her from under the outer covering of apprehension. "What's the meaning of this, Arousa?" I asked her.

"What's your name? From what country are you?" she asked me.

"My name is Qindil and I'm from the land of Islam."

"What were you asking?"

"Is he your father?" I asked, pointing outside.

"Yes."

"What relationship is there between us now?"

"My father knew that you appeal to me, so he has handed you over to me."

"Is that what is customary here?"

"Of course."

"And then what?"

"I don't know. But why do you cover your middle with that loincloth?"

She began to strip it off me, scornfully, and we stood there gazing at each other. Suddenly I knelt down, throwing off every worry, and embraced her legs to my chest.

At midday the father said to me, "Invite us to lunch."

I went and brought meat and fruit and we partook of our food like one family. After a short interval the old man said to me, "Go in peace."

"Shall I come tomorrow?" I asked him uncertainly.

"That's up to you and her," he said, unconcerned.

I returned to the inn, having lost my mind and my heart. I condensed the whole of life into Arousa. I requested more enlightenment from Fam.

"Such a relationship," he answered, "is practiced here without any reservations. No sooner does a young man appeal to a girl than she invites him in, before the eyes and ears of her family—and she'll throw him out if she gets tired of him, keeping the children, which are hers."

I hated all this from the bottom of my heart, but Fam cut in on my thoughts. "In the afternoon we shall go to the priest of the moon. He is expecting you."

My enthusiasm for the meeting had dwindled slightly, but I decided to make use of him so that I might accomplish the book of my journey as perfectly as possible. In the afternoon Fam accompanied me to the priest's tent, which was set up in an empty space. He was sitting squat-legged on a pelt in front of its entrance. He gazed at me attentively and said, "Sit down. Welcome."

When Fam had left us the priest said, "Fam has told me that you are called Qindil Muhammad al-Innabi and that you are from the land of Islam."

"That's right," I said in a friendly manner.

With his penetrating gaze directed at my chest, he said, "It's clear that you're eager to obtain information, like any foreign traveler."

"With the sage are to be found meanings that are hidden from the fleeting spectator," I said pleasantly.

"Be frank, there's no reason to be afraid, for meanings will only emerge to him who knocks at the door with sincerity."

I thought for a while, then started with the subject that engaged me. "The most extraordinary thing I have met with in Mashriq is the relationship of man with woman."

"Half, if not all, the misfortunes that happen in countries come from the heavy shackles that are placed on passion. If you are sexually satisfied, life can be contented and enjoyable."

"In our land," I said cautiously, "God orders us to act differently."

"I have learned things about your land. You have marriage and only too often it brings about distressing tragedies, and even the successful among them continue by virtue of patience. No, my friend, our life is easier and happier."

"What if the woman loses interest in her man though he is still in love with her?" I asked uneasily.

"There are many women, and finding solace is easy. All your troubles come from deprivation."

"Even an animal feels jealousy towards its partner."

He smiled. "We must be better than the animals."

Hiding my disgust, I muttered, "Our views are impossibly far apart!"

"I concede that, but you must understand us well. We search for simplicity and play. Our god does not interfere in our affairs. He says one word to us: that nothing lasts in life and that it is heading for annihilation. Thus he has pointed to the way in silence, that we might make of our lives a game and exist in contentment."

Encouraged by the heated manner in which he talked, I said, "I have heard your exhortation and find that it does not apply to the overlord who is the possessor of everything."

He shook his head sadly. "Often the thoughts of foreigners revolve round that, but it is the overlord who repels the attacks of the nomads. In him and the rest of the overlords lies our hope for resisting the ambitious desires of a land such as Haira. Yes, war threatens us, and it is the overlords who prepare themselves for our defense, and it is they too who oppose any hostility within the country and afford a safe life to the slaves. After all that, do you begrudge them that they should own everything so that they can spend money on weapons and mercenaries?"

"There's a better system which gives the people all their rights," I challenged, "and it prepares them to defend their land when necessary."

The man pouted his tightly closed lips and said peremptorily, "Creatures in our land are of four species: plants, animals, slaves, and masters; and every species has an origin different from that of the other species."

Heatedly, I said, "In our land people are brothers, from one father and one mother. There is no difference in this between the ruler and the least significant of people."

He waved his hand in scorn. "You're not the first Muslim I've talked to," he said. "I know many things about you. What you say is in truth your slogan, but is there to be found in this alleged brotherhood any trace in the way the people behave towards each other?"

This was a telling blow. "It's not a slogan but a religion," I answered passionately.

"Our religion," he scoffed, "does not claim what it does not put into practice."

His frankness shook me to my very depths. "You are a wise man and I'm amazed at how you worship the moon and imagine it to be a god."

For the first time he spoke sharply and seriously. "We see it and we understand its language. Do you see your god?"

"He is beyond mind and the senses."

"Then he is nothing," he said, smiling.

I almost slapped him, but I suppressed my rage and asked forgiveness of my Lord. "God grant you guidance," I said.

"And I ask my god to give you guidance." He smiled.

I shook him by the hand and bade him goodbye, then returned to the inn, my nerves frayed and my heart in pain. I made a pledge that in my journey I would listen much and argue little, or not at all. "Our religion is wonderful," I said to myself in grief, "but our life is pagan."

On the following day I went early to the market, to Arousa's tent. The old man greeted me with smiles and Arousa said coquettishly, "You were so late I thought you'd fled." I kissed her on the mouth, and she was about to go to our secluded corner when I stopped her and said to her father, "Father, I wish to marry Arousa."

The old man roared with laughter, disclosing where he was missing front teeth. "As you do in your country?" he said.

"Certainly, in which case I would take her along with me on my journey so that we could return together to my homeland."

The man looked at his daughter. "What do you feel, Arousa?"

Arousa said happily, "On condition he undertakes to return me to Mashriq if I want."

"I grant you that, Arousa," I said without hesitation.

"But I do not possess the right of final agreement, for we are all the slaves of the overlord and he is our legal owner. So go to the palace and propose to the chamberlain that you buy Arousa."

This obstacle, with which I had not reckoned, stood in my way, but I realized that I must without fail surmount it. I spent half the day with Arousa in deep relaxed happiness. On returning to the inn I announced to Fam what was worrying me and he promised to accompany me to the chamberlain. Thus it was decreed that I should pass through the door of the palace and view a part of its garden, resplendent with flowers and palm trees, on my way to the chamberlain. He was seated in the center of a spacious room on a large couch of rosewood, spread with soft pillows and cushions. He was over sixty, portly, with poor sight, and he was enveloped in an air of seclusion and haughtiness. Fam kissed his hand and presented my request, but the chamberlain waved his hand in a sign of refusal. "We have prohibited selling," he said, "because of our need for additional numbers of slaves." Then he looked at me. "Join us if you wish, as Fam has done, and you will be included in the general body of slaves and enjoy security, contentment, and the slave girl as well."

I thanked him for his generosity and left the palace with a heart weighed down with frustration and grief. On our way to the inn Fam said, "Enjoy your girl until you are sated—and you'll be quickly sated!" Without knowing it, he increased my sorrows. Then he went on, "The time was not opportune for making a success of your endeavors, for there is news of Haira preparing to declare war on us."

"For what reason?" I asked anxiously.

"Greed for the riches of the overlords and the rich pastures," he said, laughing bitterly. "And they will not lack a pretext for invasion."

I was assailed by anxiety and my worries increased. Near the market we parted and I went at once to Arousa's tent. I was met by the old man, who scrutinized my face. "By the moon, your efforts have been unsuccessful."

Arousa gave a meaningless laugh, and I replied sadly, "My efforts have been unsuccessful."

"She awaits you," the old man laughed, indicating Arousa.

"It pains me that my relationship with her should be transitory."

"Every relationship is transitory, stranger," mocked the old man.

"I had hoped it would be permanent!" I said fervently.

"What an egotistical traveler you are!" he said, guffawing with laughter. "Beware of complications, for we are simple people who love simplicity."

"It's as though you don't know what love is."

"We know that it is the pleasure of a night or a week, a month or a year in crazy circumstances. What do you want more than that?"

"What do you suggest for a madman like myself?" I asked seriously.

"Rent her for a renewable period."

"Shall I go back to the chamberlain for that too?"

"Not at all. That is my right as her father. What period would you like?"

"The longest possible."

"I shall rent her out month by month."

"So be it."

"But the agreement will come to an end if she so desires."

I lowered my head in agreement.

"It will be three dinars a month," he said.

The agreement was concluded and I went off with Arousa to my room at the inn. I determined not to spoil my happiness and to consider the present moment as though it were the whole of life. But I begged her to let me cover the beauty of her body. To this she replied in annoyance, "Don't make a laughingstock of me."

So I changed my mind and resigned myself to everything. She took on for me the appearance of a happy
illusion that threatened to vanish, so I joined her with a
heart pursued by the specter of separation and sadness.
And yet life became good with the wonderful young girl
and gave promise of stability and security to heart and
nerves. She loved to roam freely in the pastures and to
wander round the market, so we would go out joyfully
together. One day al-Qani ibn Hamdis saw me and approached. "We are traveling with the dawn," he said.

"But I am staying," I answered with embarrassment.

"You will find a caravan every ten days," he said,
laughing.

Immersed in love, I was not concerned with time. For
me now the journey and the important matter on which
I was engaged had no significance, even if I were to
remain here till the end of my life. Then appeared the
harbingers of motherhood with their joys of the heart
and sicknesses of the body, so I sought refuge in them
from the vicissitudes of unruly feelings and impetuous
desires. I craved a settled existence, even if it were to tie
me in the end to Mashriq and to change my whole way
of life and my dreams. "It seems," I said to myself sardon-
ically, "that I was created for love and not for journeys!"

Time passed and brought the night of the full moon,
when the people hurried off to the square of worship.
We went to the square as man and wife and squeezed

ourselves into the crowd. "This is the night of the god," she said to me solemnly, "during which husband and wife are separated."

She fled and melted into the crowds, and I remained alone, disturbed and angry, robbed of willpower and happiness. The rites were performed one after another while I asked myself what she was doing with some stranger. When the moment of embracing came I found myself facing a woman of forty possessed of a certain beauty, who opened her arms to me. It occurred to me that what was happening to me was also happening elsewhere to Arousa. Cup bearers passed round with date wine and I drank a glass. Out of my mind, I joined in the prayers of Mashriq. At dawn I collapsed and squatted at the entrance to the inn until Arousa appeared, staggering as she approached. Speechless, I went up to her and led her off to our room.

"Did you like the woman?" she asked me.

"We have dirtied a sacred relationship, Arousa," I said bitterly.

"You are not a believer, Qindil, and I can do nothing about that," she said with annoyance. Then, coming up to me with a smile, she said, "I still love you, you are still my only man."

I confess that my own love had not weakened and that fear of being separated had kindled it. She had become both my happiness and my misery.

I was scorched by the summer, which was like hellfire; all vegetation was obliterated and the cattle ate dried fodder. Autumn came, the fiery heat subsided a little, and it drizzled with rain from time to time. Then came the winter with its pleasantly mild weather and heavy rains, and the earth came to life, the cattle were delighted, and those who were naked remained naked. Arousa gave birth to her first child; he was named Ram the son of Arousa— as though she had produced him on her own and I had nothing to do with it.

Her father said to me, "Here you are entering your second year and she still loves you. Are you some magician, stranger?"

The first signs of a new motherhood broke forth and she gave birth to Aam, and a year later he was followed by Lam the son of Arousa. Then she became pregnant for the fourth time and our relationship became famous amongst the people for being exceptional: it was said that I was embracing her with a magical strength that I had learned in the lands of Islam.

Without knowing it, I was driven to bring Ram up on the principles of Islam. He was growing quicker and stronger than his companions because of the care and food I gave him, and he was put forward as an ideal of what the children of Mashriq should be, were it not for the oppression and servitude. By teaching him the principles of Islam, I expiated my inevitable neglect of my faith in deference to the country which was harboring me, though Arousa did not conceal her displeasure. "You are bringing him up in godlessness," she said seriously, "and preparing him for a life of misery in his own country."

"I am saving his soul," I said gently, "just as I once had hoped to save yours."

"I shall never permit you to do that," she said severely.

She showed herself so stubbornly that I grew fearful for my love. She disclosed her worries to her father when we were on a visit to him. He was greatly upset and shouted at me, "Keep away from our son, stranger."

It seemed that the news leaked out, despite our having kept it to ourselves, and looks of anger seared me as I walked in the street. Pursued by feelings of unease, I told myself, "The building is threatened with collapse."

My conjectures were correct, for Fam came and took me from my room to his own, where I found a police officer waiting for me.

"Are you Qindil Muhammad al-Innabi?" he asked.

"Yes," I answered, my mouth dry.

"It has been established that you are trying to bring up your eldest son to godlessness," he said sternly.

"How has that been established?" I asked in alarm.

"We know best how to perform our duty. Listen, for I have not come to discuss things with you: the overlord's order has been issued that you should be separated from your mistress and her children and that you should depart from Mashriq with the first caravan."

I was about to speak, but he said roughly, "I did not come to talk. You are under arrest so that they may take the woman and the children to her father. You shall remain under guard until you join the caravan."

"Let me say goodbye to them," I pleaded.

"You have received the most lenient punishment, so be grateful," he said gruffly.

An hour later I returned to my room, which had been turned into a prison. I found it empty of mother and children, of love and hope. A moment of gloom spread over the depths of my soul, and life stripped away the veil from a dream and an illusion. Fam joined me, gazing at me with sympathy. "Put up with it as befits a man who is a traveler."

"I am distraught, Fam," I said, my voice shaking.

He scrutinized my face for a while, then said, "Let your tears flow—men sometimes cry."

Trying to control my tears, I said, "The pleasures of life have evaporated."

"They will be renewed and will come with solace."

He patted me on the shoulder and said, "You must know that a traveler should not strive after a permanent relationship."

3

The Land of Haira

The caravan moved off in a darkness that betrayed the
first glimpses of dawn. My heart was pulled backwards,
my throat was tight with sadness and tears. The stars
were grouped above us, they looking at us and we at
them, and all solace was absent. Just as I had left my
homeland some five years before, frustrated by the be-
trayal of mother, of sweetheart, and of those in power,
so once again I had turned into a traveler thinking of
countries and notebooks—but where was the heart, the
mind? These stars, I told myself, were nearer to me than
Arousa and the children. Caravans continue to make their
way carrying riches and hopes. Who, though, carries
sorrows? The darkness vanishes and light shines, and the
desert shows itself without boundaries, like extinction. I
wondered what they were saying about me back home,
and why I had not again come across al-Qani ibn Hamdis.
I told myself, "The best thing you can do, traveler, is to
see and hear and record and to shun experiences, to re-
sume your dreams of the land of Gebel, and to bear off

healing remedies for the wounds of your mother country."

We traversed the distance between Mashriq and Haira in one month, and made camp in the vicinity of the Zemam Oasis, so that we might enter Haira at midnight. With nightfall we continued on our way until there loomed before us the town walls under the light of the stars, and we drew nearer to its great gateway.

In front of the entrance, in the light of torches, stood the director of customs. It seemed, from his helmet, breastplate, sword, and short loincloth, that he was a military man. He spoke in a strong voice that carried to the whole of the caravan. "Welcome to Haira, capital of the land of Haira. Everywhere here you will find policemen, so ask them about what you want. By following their instructions precisely you will make of your journey a pleasant memory with nothing to spoil it."

"Both a welcome and a warning," I thought.

We went through the gateway, then divided up, the traders going to the market inn, while a guide took me off to the inn of the foreigners. We went through pitch-darkness, in which floated here and there like stars the torches of the policemen. As we approached the inn I saw its great entrance in the light of the flares, and light shone from some of the windows. A large stone building, it consisted of a single story. I quickly made my way behind my traveling bags, which were being borne off to my room. The room was of medium size and contained a bed that stood a cubit from the floor; this had a purple covering well suited to the mild autumnal weather. There was also a cupboard for clothes, a small sofa, and a candelabrum. In an aperture in the center of the candelabrum burned a thick candle. The floor was covered by an elaborately designed rug. Civilization was, no doubt, to be found here. What a difference between this and Mashriq!

I had hardly got out of my traveling clothes and put on my nightgown when there appeared a brown-skinned man of medium height. He was in his fifties and wore a thin cloak.

"I'm Ham," he said, "owner of the inn."

I shook him by the hand. "Qindil Muhammad al-Innabi, traveler."

"Do you want supper?"

"I had it on the way."

"The night, board and lodging," he said with a smile, "is one dinar. Payment in advance."

I estimated that my stay would extend to ten days, so I handed him ten dinars.

"From what country are you?" he asked me.

"From the land of Islam."

"Here," he said cautioningly, "only the religion of Haira is practiced."

This reminded me of my tragedy in Mashriq, and I asked him, "And what is the religion of Haira?"

"Our god is the king." At this he bade me farewell and left.

I blew out the candle, then went to bed, saying to myself, "After the moon, now the king. What delusion and error! But let me not be hasty. Does not the ruler in my own homeland act like a god? Enjoy repose after the hardships of the journey and take refuge in sleep from all the troubles of life."

I woke earlier than I had expected and at once realized that it was a great noise erupting in the street that had wrenched me from my slumbers. Opening a window, I saw by the light of early day that a huge army—cavalry and foot soldiers—was advancing towards the city gate to the beating of drums. I watched and wondered what it was about. When the street had emptied I asked for breakfast, and I was brought a brass tray of milk, butter, cheese, and bread, with a bunch of grapes. I was about to inquire of the servant about the passing of the army but I was constrained by caution. I put on my clothes to go out and found the entrance jam-packed with people, all deep in discussion.

"It's war, just as many had expected."

"Against Mashriq without doubt."

"To liberate a people from five tyrants."

"It will mean a new history for Mashriq under the rule of a just god."

I was depressed, and my thoughts took flight to hover around Arousa and her children. What would their fate be? It was not the desire to liberate the people of Mashriq that had driven Haira to war but greed for pastures and the treasures of the five overlords. Harsh coercion would be employed to transform the people from worshipers of the moon to worshipers of the king. Spirits would be stifled to death, reputations torn to shreds, and thousands made homeless. Does that not happen even in wars that break out between peoples with a single religion calling for unity and brotherhood? Ham came to me before I left. "It has been decided to raise the daily rate to one and a half dinars in order to meet the burdens of the war."

I paid over the difference grudgingly and he said, smiling, "It is not much to pay in the cause of freeing slaves."

Secretly I cursed him just as I have cursed all false slogans. Deeply disquieted, I went to the market inn, where I found my merchant companions gathered in the hallway. I sat down with them and followed their conversation.

"Days of war are insecure."

"Our wealth may be lost to the last dirham."

"But prices will also rise."

"And the extra toll dues?"

"Wars never cease," said the owner of the caravan, "and their benefit to trade is greater than their harm. I do not imagine that this war will go on for very long, for Haira is immeasurably stronger than Mashriq. Everything will be over in less than a week."

My thoughts became concentrated on my missing family and I decided to stay on in Haira, close to Mashriq. I was enticed by a new hope—namely, that after Mashriq was joined to Haira I would be able to travel to Mashriq, where God might, in His mercy and kindness, unite me with my family. Perhaps I would be able to marry Arousa and continue, together with her, on my journey to a new home and a new religion. My life became agreeable with this new hope, and my heart grew joyful at making the rounds of Haira and exploring its capital city.

I walked around it tirelessly, looking and listening and recording everything in my memory. It was a city like those of my own country: it had squares and gardens, streets and alleyways, great structures, houses, schools, and hospitals; it was teeming with people, and everywhere there were policemen, while places of dancing and singing were plentiful. Its market was large and extensive with numerous booths, exhibiting goods from Haira itself and from all countries. The mild autumnal weather induced in me limitless energy, and so the days of discovering and viewing and recording continued. From time to time I would visit the market inn and meet my companions, or sit with the owner of the caravan, who once said to me, "The weather of Haira is in general mild; its summer is bearable and its winter reasonable."

When I spoke to him about the great number of policemen, he said, "Security is assured, they are protecting the state."

I walked round the districts inhabited by the rich, which are beautiful and tranquil; their palaces are museums, and their inhabitants move about in sedan chairs. I also visited the poor quarters, with their huts, ruins, mournful atmosphere, and miserable people. I spoke of this to the owner of the caravan. "They claim that the war was started in order to free the slaves in Mashriq. Why don't they free the slaves of Haira?"

The man inquired in a whisper, "And what have you to say about our country, the country of divine Revelation?"

"There is no evil I have come across in my journey which has not reminded me of my unhappy country," I said sorrowfully.

"You should have a look at the palace of the god-king," the man said as he moved off.

I did not neglect to do this. I found it standing there mighty and lofty in its isolation amidst a space walled in by palm trees and guards. It was like the palace of the ruler in my homeland, yet even finer. The barracks of the guards were alongside it, while the temple of the god-king was on the other side. My gaze was drawn to a field of poles surrounded by an iron fence. When I approached I saw that human heads were fixed to the tops of the poles. I gave a shudder at the ghastly sight. They were exhibiting the heads as a warning to offenders. Approaching a guard, I asked him, "May a stranger know what was the crime of these executed people?"

"Insurrection against the god-king," he answered gruffly.

Extending my thanks to him, I went off, certain that they were martyrs to justice and liberty, deducing this from what usually occurs in the land of divine Revelation. This is a strange world, replete with madness, and it will be truly a miracle if I find the palliative in the land of Gebel. In the evening I asked Ham, "What sights of Haira should be seen besides those of the capital?"

"Apart from the capital," the man said confidently, "there is nothing but the countryside, and it has nothing to attract the traveler."

I devoted myself to noting down the sights, which released me from thinking about Arousa and her children. One evening I spent in a nightclub and was shocked at the uproar of the drunks and the depravity which my pen refrains from recounting. As I passed by the market inn the owner of the caravan said to me, "We are traveling tomorrow at dawn—are you coming with us?"

Glumly I responded, "No, I'm staying a while."

The thought of Arousa induced me to remain, but I

was pained by the frightful loneliness that awaited me. At dawn I woke and imagined the caravan moving off to the singing of the leader. Yet a call like destiny was inviting me to stay on, a hope for happiness which did not want to die out. I had no wish to waste my time in vain, so I actively went around gathering information which was not to be gained by sightseeing. I found that the owner of the inn, unlike the one I had met in Mashriq, had no spare time in which to converse, so I asked him to conduct me to the sage of this land, to see if he would grant me an interview.

"It is possible for me to arrange an interview for you, as has happened with others," Ham said.

In the afternoon I went to the appointment at the house of the sage Daizing; a beautiful house surrounded by a garden filled with flowers and fruit trees. He greeted me with a pleasant smile and sat me down on a couch alongside him. In his fifties, he was of strong build with distinct features, his white skullcap matching his white cloak. He asked me to say something about myself, so I mentioned my name, my mission, and my homeland.

"Your country is also great," he said. "Tell me, what has appealed to you about our land?"

Hiding my real thoughts, I said, "Innumerable things —civilization and beauty, power and organization."

"What do you think of our declaration of war, sacrificing our sons to liberate a foreign land?" he asked proudly.

"This is something we have not heard of before."

"We present people with a model for an honorable and happy homeland," he said with conviction. I bowed my head in agreement, and he said, "Perhaps you ask yourself what the secret is in all this? They have conducted you to me because I am the sage of this country. The truth is that I am no more than a pupil. Our Majesty is the sage, and he is the god, and he is the source of all wisdom and good. He sits on the throne, then isolates himself in a wing of the palace, fasting until light radiates from him. Then he knows that the god has alighted upon him and that he has become the adored godhead. Thereupon he exercises his function, seeing everything with the eye of the god, and thus we receive from him everlasting wisdom in everything, after which nothing is demanded of us but to have faith and obey."

I followed him attentively, as I inwardly asked forgiveness of my Lord.

"It is he who organizes the army, and chooses its commanders to assure it of victory," he continued. "He appoints the governors from his holy family, and picks leaders for the work on the land and in the factories from amongst the elite. As for the rest of the people, they possess no sanctity and have no talents; they do manual work and we provide them with their daily bread. After them come the animals, and after the animals the plants and inanimate things—a complete and precise system that puts each individual in his place, thus achieving the most perfect justice."

He was silent for a while as he looked at me, then he said, "We thus possess more than one philosophy. We talk to the elite in terms that will strengthen the power, control, and growth that is in their souls, helping them therein by providing them with educational and medical facilities. As for the others, we strengthen in them the gifts of obedience, compliance, and contentment, leading them to the spiritual treasure that is buried within each one of them and which provides them with patience, application, and peace. With this twofold philosophy happiness for all is assured, each in accordance with his disposition and what has been set aside for him, for we are without exception the happiest people in the whole world."

Having given thought to what had been said and what had not been said, I asked him, "Who owns the land and the factories?"

"The god, who is the creator and the king."

"And the elite?"

"They are the owners by proxy, the income being divided equally between them and the god."

"How is the god's wealth spent?" I inquired, making a new leap.

He laughed, for the first time, and said, "Is a god to be asked about what he does?"

"Then who spends on the schools and hospitals?"

"The elite, seeing it as an obligation to be discharged by them and their children." He then demanded proudly, "Isn't this perfection itself?"

Dissembling, I said, "That is what is usually said of the land of Gebel."

"The land of Haira *is* the land of Gebel," he shouted.

"You are quite right, sage Daizing!" I declared.

He spoke with confidence and conviction. "To live with guidance from the god is man's highest aspiration in terms of happiness and justice."

"It is for this reason," I put in, "that I am astonished by those rebellious people whose heads I saw strung up!"

"Human nature is not free from disorder and evil," he exclaimed angrily, "but such are a minority in any case."

At the end of our meeting he offered me an apple and a glass of milk and I returned, with my sad thoughts, to my solitude in the inn. I remembered my master, Sheikh Maghagha al-Gibeili, and asked, "Who is worse, Master, he who claims divinity through ignorance or he who exploits the Quran for his own ends?"

I endured boredom for several days, then news reached me, spread by the autumnal breezes, confirming that Haira's army had been victorious; it had achieved its aims and the land of Mashriq had become the northern province of Haira. The poor poured into the streets to announce their joy at the victory—as though it were they who would reap its fruits.

"I wonder how you are, Arousa," I said to myself, greatly troubled. "And my children."

On the day of the return of the victorious army I got up early and took up my position not far from the inn on the royal route that stretched from the entrance to Haira right up to the king's palace. The crush on both sides of the route was so extreme that it seemed not a single citizen had stayed at home or at work. Just before noon the sound of drumbeats reached our ears. The procession was led by horsemen bearing on their spears five heads— the heads of the five overlords who had held sway over the cities of Mashriq. Thus I saw for the first time the overlord to whose chamberlain I had gone to bargain for the purchase of Arousa. There followed a long line of prisoners of war, walking naked with fettered hands between ranks of guards. There then came detachments of horse and foot soldiers, to boisterous cheering. It was a day of victory and festivities. Only God knew about the bloody tragedies that it had left behind. A strange human existence that can be summed up in two words: blood and rejoicing.

In the rear of the army amidst guards walked the women captives. My heart beat wildly as I formed the image of Arousa, seeing her as I had seen her the first time—or rather as I had seen her leading her father in the lane which witnessed my birth. My gaze roamed among the downcast faces and naked bodies, and my yearning came true as my eyes fell upon Arousa's face: Arousa, with her slender body and unhappy, handsome face, approaching dazed, desperate, and wretched. A storming burst of energy broke out in me. I rushed forward, following in the wake of the line of captives, mindless of the bystanders against whom I knocked, or of their protests and their accusations that I was running after the naked bodies of the women. I called to her over and over but my cry was lost in the din of rising voices and I failed to attract her attention. I was even barred from her by the guards, who prevented the crowds from entering the palace square, which was reserved for Haira's elite. Thus it was that she came to view and then vanished like a meteor, leaving me to madness and despair. And where were the children? Were they now living under the protection of their grandfather? I eased my distress by divulging my secret to Ham, who said, "She may be put up for sale in the slave market."

"But it was a war of liberation," I said in disbelief.

"Except for captives of war, who receive special treatment," he said.

I invoked a blessing on this piece of hypocrisy: it was a peephole of hope in a sky of blackness. I clung even tighter to the idea of remaining on, and began to roam around the slave market every day, my dream of being reunited challenging my despair. Then one evening Ham met me with an encouraging smile. "Tomorrow the captives are being put up for sale."

I slept badly that night, and when I went to the market I was the first to arrive. When Arousa was put up for sale I entered into the auction with determination. For the first time in her life she was dressed in a robe—it was green—and her beauty revealed itself despite her deep sadness. She was looking into her shattered self and did not see me, nor did she follow what was going on. The only person left in the bidding was, I heard it whispered, the representative of the sage Daizing. She was knocked down to me for thirty dinars, and when she was brought to me she recognized me and fell into my arms sobbing, to the astonishment of all those in the market. There was no opportunity of conversing, so I took her outside. On the way I could not help asking her, "How are the children, Arousa?"

However, because of her nervous state of agitation I forbore from pressing her until we were alone in my room at the inn. There I clasped her to me warmly, then set her on the couch until she was herself again. Then I said, "I grieve at the distress you have suffered."

"But you saw nothing," she said in a strange voice.

"Tell me, Arousa, for I am almost mad with despair."

"About what?" she said, her eyes streaming with tears.

"It was ghastly. They rushed into the tent and killed my father for no reason and seized me. Where are the children? I don't know. Were they killed? Lost? Leave madness to me!"

Battling my fears, I said, "Why should they kill the little ones? They're somewhere—we'll find them."

"They are savages—why should they torture us after defeating our army? But they are savages. It was the night of the full moon and the god was present, seeing and hearing but doing nothing."

"In any case we are reunited," I said consolingly, "and my heart tells me that mercy is on the way."

"There is no mercy," she exclaimed, "and I shall not see my children again."

"Arousa," I said, hopefully, "there is much evil in life, but good abounds too."

"I don't believe it."

"You'll see—we'll go with the first caravan to Mashriq to search for the children."

"When does it set out?"

"Within ten days."

She gazed blankly with deep sadness and my heart overflowed with tenderness like a bubbling spring of water. We amused ourselves during our long empty wait by wandering round the city and seeing the sights, ruminating over our hopes and preparing for our journey. Ham, however, was holding in reserve a surprise for us.

Inviting me to his room, he looked at me with a certain embarrassment and said, "I have some unpleasant news."

"More than I already have?" I asked bitterly.

"The sage Daizing wishes to have possession of your woman."

I was astonished. "I hope you regard her as my wife," I replied heatedly.

"He'll pay you her price."

"She's not a commodity."

"Daizing is a powerful man and close to the god," he said in the tone of someone giving friendly advice.

Hiding my confusion, I said, "But strangers in your country live in security."

"My opinion about your position in this matter will not change," he retorted.

I was at a loss. Should I tell Arousa of the conversation? Should I add yet another sorrow to those she endured? In truth I was worried about disturbing the delight she had in the one dream that remained to her. I asked myself whether Daizing was able, through his influence, to tear Arousa away from me. I recollected the Sultan's chamberlain who had stolen Halima from me in my homeland. I did not arrive at a firm opinion that set my mind at rest. All the while I was conscious of a danger pursuing me, that my happiness neither was firmly based nor yet had wings. Four days before we were due to depart, a servant asked me to go to see Ham in his room. There I found a police officer, to whom Ham presented me. "You will come with me to meet the chief of the city's police," he said.

I demanded the reason and he pretended not to know. I asked that I might inform Arousa, but the officer said, "Ham will do that for you."

We went to the general police department on the Royal Road and I appeared before the director, who sat on a couch, surrounded by assistants. With a glance that gave me no reassurance, he asked, "You are Qindil Muhammad al-Innabi, the traveler?"

I answered that I was and he said, "You are accused of ridiculing the religion of this land whose hospitality you are enjoying."

"An accusation without any basis of truth," I answered vehemently.

"There are witnesses," he said coldly.

"No one with any conscience can give such evidence," I exclaimed.

"Don't defame innocent people," he said, "and leave that to the judge's assessment."

And so I was arrested, and the following morning I was taken to court. The charge was read out and I denied it. Five witnesses came along, at the head of them Ham, and after taking the oath, they all gave the same evidence, as though they had learned it by heart. The court sentenced me to be imprisoned for life, and my belongings were confiscated. Thus it was that Arousa was taken into custody. All this happened between one day and the next. I experienced the taste of bitter despair and realized that what had happened was for real, not a story being re-counted. Arousa was lost, the journey was thwarted, the dream of the land of Gebel was dissipated, my very existence in this world was nullified.

The prison was on the outskirts of the city in a desert area. It consisted of a vast space under the ground, with narrow apertures in the ceiling, walls of large stones, and a sandy floor. Each prisoner had nothing but a pair of trousers and an animal pelt; the atmosphere choked in a turbid stench in the twilight on which no sun rose. Looking around me aghast, I said to myself, "I shall remain here till the last day of my life!" My companions stared and asked me about my crime. They asked me, and I asked back in turn. I realized that what brought us together were political and doctrinal crimes. I found a certain consolation in that, if someone in my position could find any solace. They were an unusual group of liberals who had been oppressed by the corrupt environment. They heard my story and one of them commented on it with the words "Even foreigners!"

Not one of them had expressed disbelief in the god, this being a crime for which the punishment was decapitation. But they questioned critically some of the anomalous actions pertaining to justice and human freedom. Among them I saw an old man of more than eighty years: he had spent fifty of them in prison, having begun his term in the reign of the previous king. I saw that he had lost his senses and his mind: he did not know where he was or why he had been brought here. His weak body, a body without spirit, spent its days prostrate on his pelt.

"Of us all he is the most deserving of felicitation," a voice said.

Without hesitation I felt the words to be true.

Our thoughts revolved round man's position in this world.

"There is no happy country."

"Suffering is the common human language."

"We the bewildered stand between ugly reality and the dream that never comes true."

"But there are countries that are better."

"Even they do not yet know contentment."

"And the land of Gebel?"

At the mention of the magic name my heart gave a bound and I remembered with pain my lost objective. "What do you know about it?" I asked.

"No more than is usually said: that it is the land of perfection."

"Haven't you read any books about it or met any of those who have visited it?" I asked.

"No, there is nothing but hearsay."

"And who will make the dream come true?"

"Man—none but man."

I was tired of words, tired of enduring my sorrows, tired of lying hopes.

"There is no world for me," I thought, "except this everlasting prison."

In my perpetual prison, I found no benefit in the rational thinking of my master, Sheikh Maghagha, but I did find a certain ease to my despair in my mother's naïve philosophy of predestination, as though it were a philosophy specially created for life imprisonment. I capitulated. "Let it be the will of God, for everything that comes to me is from Him." I gave myself over to my fate. I buried my hopes. I bade final farewell to my past, my present, and my future. The sole remaining hope for a prisoner like myself was to kill hope, and to come to terms with the grave which had swallowed me, and to take to wife deep-rooted, all-controlling, and pervasive despair. Specters of the homeland, of my mother, of Arousa and the children, and of the land of Gebel followed one upon another. I became habituated to the turbid smell, for no smell existed except it; to the faint, semi-dark light, for there was no light in the universe except it; and to the ever-present insects, for they were in control of the place and had priority there, while pain and boredom were one's constant companions. I went on drowning in depths that had no end. Silence reigned and torment was changed into a habit, and I derived from despair extraordinary power to endure and persevere. A voice would pierce through the wall of silence: "It is related of a prisoner of ancient times that he generated in himself such an extraordinary power that he was able to penetrate the prison wall, like a voice, and to fly in the air beyond all boundaries."

My patience would accept this raving gladly, and after a day or a year another voice said, "War may break out between Haira and Halba. Then we shall once again ascend to the earth's surface."

So I forgive those on the earth's surface who testified against me and I ask myself when, like the happy old man, I shall lose my senses. I descended into the depths step by step, so that time was lost, as the mainstays of life were lost, and history vanished. I became ignorant of what hour it was, what day, what month, what year: the appearances of times disappeared, my life became an enigma. I began growing older without limitation, without calculation, and there was no mirror in which to see myself, only my comrades to help me imagine how ugly and filthy I had become. Nobody knew happiness in our world except the vermin and insects. Doubtless eras, epochs, and ages were succeeding one another, while we savored the taste of extinction in its eternal sublimity.

And so it went on and on and on until a new arrival was hurled in amongst us. Like vermin we gathered round him, looking with amazement at the newcomer from the other world. Despite his great age and wretchedness it seemed to me that I was not seeing him for the first time. The old man had died a time ago, we knew not how long ago, and this person had come to replace him. He looked into our faces and wept.

"Don't cry, man," someone said, "for tears harm the vermin."

"Who are you?" someone asked.

"I am the sage Daizing," he answered mournfully.

I emerged from my everlasting trance and shouted in a strange voice, "Daizing . . . Daizing . . . How could I forget you!"

"And who are you?" he asked.

"I am your victim," I called out, falling back into that time.

"We have found ourselves in the same calamity," he said entreatingly.

"Not at all—we are not the same," I shouted.

"The world has been turned upside down," he called out. "The commander of the army has rebelled against the king and replaced him."

Life crept back into my comrades and a tremor of enthusiasm emanated from them. "What is happening on the earth's surface?" one of them inquired.

"The king's men have been killed. As for me, I was condemned to life imprisonment."

The empty sticks of men were filled with a new hope

and cheers arose for the new god. As for me, I asked him savagely, "And don't you remember me?"

"Who are you?" he asked fearfully.

"I am the owner of Arousa," I exclaimed. "Do you remember me now?"

He backed away warily and lowered his head.

"What happened to her, you scoundrel?"

"We tried to make our escape in the caravan going to the land of Halba," he said meekly, "but they arrested me, while she traveled on to Halba."

"What about her children?"

"We had traveled together to Mashriq to look for them, but we found no trace of them. That happened a long time ago."

While, like much else, I had forgotten my sorrows, my anger increased. "You are no sage," I shouted. "Nothing but a vile scoundrel! You did not hesitate to trump up an accusation so as to steal my wife. To be done to death is too mild a punishment for you!"

The voice of the guard came down to me from an aperture in the ceiling, ordering me to keep away from him, so I went back to my place, my weak body collapsing under the sudden gush of life that had swept over it. I sat down on my pelt, with my back against the wall and my legs stretched out, taking in once again the movement of life and of history. I would have liked to ask him how long I had spent in prison, but I disliked the idea of continuing my conversation with him. However, he looked towards me and said sadly, "I'm sorry. I feel remorse for what I did."

"The likes of you are not worthy of remorse," I said bitterly.

"I had my punishment," he said in the same tone, "by living with a woman who didn't for a moment stop hating me." Then, as though talking to himself: "For twenty years she did not change the feelings of her heart."

Twenty years! A life lost! The answer came to me with the cutting cruelty of the blade of a dagger. Here was the traveler sinking down into his middle forties. One day he would die in this tomb having achieved no goal, enjoyed no pleasure, performed no duty. My depression was further increased by having this scoundrel with me in the tomb to remind me of the setbacks I had suffered, my bad luck, and my failure to achieve my goals. As for my comrades, they became ablaze with a new hope, all of them expecting that at any moment a comprehensive pardon would be issued. In fact their hopes did not go unanswered, for one day the governor of the prison came and said, "The will of the new god has required that a general pardon be issued for the victims of the deposed and false king."

We all stood up and shouted our good wishes and support for the king. We left the prison—all, that is, except for Daizing. Outside, the light of day was painful after the long darkness, so we shielded our eyes with the palms of our hands. An officer took me to the central office for foreigners, where the manager said, "We are sorry for the injustice that you have suffered and which is at odds with the principles and laws of the land of Haira. It has been decided to return your property to you—except for the slave girl, who has left the country."

I at once made my way to the public baths, where they shaved the hair off my head and body and where I washed with warm water and anointed myself from head to foot with balsam oil to rid myself of the bugs and vermin. I then went to the inn of the foreigners, looking forward to an emotional meeting with Ham. It appeared, though, that the man had died and that he had been replaced by someone called Tad, who was his cousin and had married his daughter. A truly emotional meeting did take place, though not between Ham and me but between me and myself in the mirror. I saw there Qindil the middle-aged man, resurrected from the grave after being buried there for twenty years: a clean-shaven middle-aged man, thin and lackluster, with sunken eyes, a gloomy complexion, lifeless look, and prominent cheekbones. I immediately decided to stay on in Haira in order to regain my health, strength, and inner harmony. I went off for a walk, not with the object of seeing what was new but in order to get my legs back into training.

I began to ask myself what I should do: Should I return

to my homeland, content simply with returning though without anything to show for my journey? Or should I continue on my voyage of exploration, rapping on the doors of fate? I disliked the idea of returning home in this state of desolate failure. My heart told me that back home I was considered dead, and that no one awaited me or was concerned about my return—that is, if death had not already overtaken them and torn out their roots and sown strangeness and estrangement in their place. No, I would not return. I would not look backwards. I had started as a traveler and as a traveler I would continue on my way. It was both decision and destiny, both vision and action, both beginning and end. To the land of Halba and thence beyond, right to the land of Gebel. I wonder, Arousa, how you look today, a woman in your forties.

4

The Land of Halba

As in days past the caravan moved off with unhurried majesty. We plunged into the gentle darkness of dawn, not this time to drink deeply of poetry but to relive the blows from memories of prison, the sorrows of a wasted life. When I saw the shapes of my companions, it was a new generation of traders that I was viewing, but energy still persisted, wealth increased, and honor and glory still stalked the adventurous. As for the dreamers, perplexity was for them. My former failures passed before me: the moment I had quit my homeland, mourning Halima, the moment I had been turned out of Mashriq, weeping for Arousa, and the moment I had said farewell to Haira, bemoaning the loss of happiness and youth. I became aware of the east and saw it surging with red rosewater, while the face of the sun, as had been its habit throughout these past twenty years, swelled forth. The desert revealed itself as endless, and summer unloaded its heat. We continued our journey for about a month. At one of the rest stops I asked the owner of the caravan about al-Qani ibn Hamdis, and he said, "God rest his soul." I then asked about Sheikh Maghagha al-Gibeili, but he had not heard of him, nor had any of the traders in the caravan.

We made camp at Shama, preparatory to entering Halba. My hair and beard had begun to grow and healthy blood was again running in my veins. We continued on our way until we saw the great walls in the lunar light.

The director of customs advanced towards us. He wore a light jacket suited to the mild summer weather. "Welcome to Halba," he said joyfully, "the capital of the land of Halba, the land of freedom."

I was amazed to hear the accursed word wherever I went; I was amazed too that his words were devoid of any warning note, declared or hidden.

"The first land to welcome the newcomer without a warning," I said to the owner of the caravan.

"It's the land of freedom," he answered, laughing, "but as a foreigner your security lies in being on your guard."

They took me off to the inn for guests. On the way, under the light of the moon, the city's landmarks were scattered in a grandeur that suggested a new panorama. So too did the great number of sedan chairs coming and going in the light of flares at such a late hour. The entrance to the inn stood erect, broad, and tall under a roofed gallery from which hung candelabra that dazzled the eyes. The building itself looked high and vast, beautifully and richly constructed. My room gave me another surprise, with its blue walls, sumptuous carpet, raised brass bedstead with its embroidered coverings, and other things usually to be found only in upper-class houses in my homeland. It disclosed to me eloquently a civilization without doubt very many degrees superior to that of Haira. I found myself wondering where and how Arousa was now living. Before I had immersed myself in my memories, I was paid a visit by a middle-aged man wearing a blue jacket and short white trousers. "Qalsham," he said to me, smiling, "the manager of the inn."

I introduced myself to him and he inquired politely if there was anything he could do for me.

"Nothing before I go to sleep now," I said frankly, "except to let me know the rates for staying here."

"Three dinars the night," he said, smiling.

I was horrified at the figure and told myself that everything in Halba appeared to enjoy freedom, including the prices. As usual, I paid for ten nights in advance.

I went to bed, and not since leaving my homeland did I enjoy so welcoming a one. I rose early and breakfast was brought to me in my room; it consisted of bread, milk, cheese, butter, honey, and eggs. I was astonished by both the quality and the quantity of the food and was ever more convinced that I was visiting a new and exciting world. Leaving the room, I was stirred by heartfelt longings and by the hope that I might also come across Arousa, so that destiny's game might be completed. Qalsham met me at the entrance to the inn. "Sedan chairs are available to the traveler for seeing the important sights," he said.

I thought a while, then said, "I'd like to start on my own and take it as it comes."

From the first instant I felt I was in a city so large that the individual melted into anonymity. In front of the inn was a vast square, on the surrounds of which stood buildings and shops; at the far end, in the middle, there was a bridge across a river leading to a small square from which large streets branched out, stretching away endlessly, their sides bordered by buildings and trees. Where was I bound for? Where was Arousa to be found? How could I proceed without a guide? I allowed my feet to lead me freely in this city of freedom, and I was enchanted by all that met my gaze at every step. A network of streets without beginning or end, rank upon rank of buildings: houses, palaces, shops as numerous as the desert sands exhibiting countless varieties of goods, factories, places of business, and places of entertainment. There were numerous parks of every kind and description, and endless streams of men and women and sedan chairs: the rich and the great, and the poor too, though these were several degrees better off than the poor of Haira and Mashriq; and not a street without a mounted policeman. The clothes of the men and the women were varied, and beauty and elegance were much in evidence. Modesty was to be found alongside emancipation that was close to nakedness, while seriousness and gravity went hand in hand with gaiety and simplicity. It was as if I were meeting for the first time human beings who had their own existence, their significance, their pride in themselves. But how could a person hope to come across Arousa in this raging sea without shores? I walked, grew tired, and rested in the parks, feeling all the time that I had not yet started. I regretted that I had not taken one of the sedan chairs for travelers that Qalsham had mentioned.

However, I saw two interesting incidents. The first was an isolated incident in a public park, when I saw policemen questioning some people; I then learned that the gardener had come across the body of a murdered woman in a corner of the park. Similar things often occur everywhere. The second thing I saw, though, aroused my disconcerted astonishment: the passing of a demonstration of men and women shouting their demands, while the police followed them without interfering in any way. I recollected a similar demonstration I had witnessed in my homeland, which was on its way to the Sultan to complain about increased taxes and the straitened material situation. But this demonstration was demanding legal recognition of homosexual relations. I could believe neither my eyes nor my ears. I was convinced I was going around in a strange world and that a vast chasm separated me from it, and I was overcome by fear of the unknown.

Noontime approached and the temperature rose to its highest. Nonetheless, Halba's summer was bearable. I was asking the way back to the inn when a voice rang out with the words "God is greatest!"

My heart jumped violently, kindling a fire in my senses. Good Lord, this was a muezzin giving the call to prayers! Did this mean that Halba was a Muslim country? Guided by the direction of the voice, I rushed off until I found a mosque at the entrance to a street. I had not heard such a sound or seen such a sight for a quarter of a century. I was being born anew, and it was as though I were discovering God for the first time. I entered the mosque, made my ablutions, and, taking my place in the ranks of those praying, I performed the noon prayer with a glowing joy, a tearful eye, and a happy heart. When the prayers were over the people left, but I stood pinned to the ground till there was no one left in the mosque but the imam and I. I hurried towards him and clasped him in my arms, kissing him on both cheeks warmly. He submitted to my enthusiasm, quietly smiling, then muttered, "Welcome, stranger."

We sat down not far from the mihrab and introduced ourselves. He was Sheikh Hamada al-Sabki, a true native inhabitant of Halba. Breathlessly, my voice shaking, I said, "I didn't imagine that Halba was a Muslim country."

"Halba is not a Muslim country," he said gently. Having read my astonishment, he added, "Halba is a free country. All religions are to be found in it. It has Muslims, Jews, Christians, and Buddhists; in fact it also has atheists and pagans."

"How has this come about, Master?" I asked, my astonishment increased.

"Halba was originally heathen," he said simply, "and its state of freedom gave to all who wanted it the opportunity of propagating their religion. The various religions spread among its people, so that today there is only a minority of heathens in some of the oases."

"What religion does the state observe?" I asked with increasing interest.

"The state has nothing to do with religion."

"How, then, are the different creeds and sects reconciled?"

"All are treated on the basis of complete equality," he said simply.

"And are they content with that?" I asked him, as though remonstrating against it.

"Every faith preserves within itself its own traditions, and mutual respect rules social relations, no distinction being given to any one faith, even if the head of state is of it. Talking of which, I would inform you that our present head is heathen."

An astonishing and thought-provoking country!

"A freedom of which I have never previously heard," I said thoughtfully. "Are you aware, Master, of the demonstration demanding legal recognition of homosexual relations?"

"It also contained Muslims," he said, smiling.

"They are no doubt penalized by their coreligionists."

The sheikh removed his turban and rubbed his hand across his head, then put it back and said, "Freedom is the sacred value accepted by everyone."

I protested. "This freedom has overstepped the boundaries of Islam."

"But it is also sacred in the Islam of Halba."

Frustrated, I said, "If our Prophet were to be resurrected today he would reject this side of your Islam."

"And were he, may the blessings and peace of God be upon him, to be resurrected," he in turn inquired, "would he not reject the whole of your Islam?"

Ah, the man had spoken the truth and had humbled me by his question.

"I have traveled much through the lands of Islam," the imam said.

"It was for this purpose," I said sadly, "that I undertook my journey, Sheikh Hamada. I wanted to see my homeland from afar, and to see it in the light of other lands, that I might perhaps be able to say something of benefit to it."

"You have done well," said Sheikh Hamada approvingly. "May God grant you success. You will be taking from our land more than one lesson."

"If you will permit, we shall have other opportunities of exchanging views," I said, taken up again by a traveler's curiosity. "But for now, could you tell me about the system of government in this extraordinary land?"

"It's a unique system," said Sheikh Hamada. "You have not met it in anything you've seen, and you will not meet it in what you will yet see."

"Not even in the land of Gebel?"

"I know nothing about the land of Gebel to be able to make the comparison. What you should know is that the head of our state is elected in accordance with political, moral, and scientific specifications. He rules for a period of ten years, after which he retires and is replaced by the chief judge. New elections are then held between the retired head of state and the new nominees."

"A good system," I exclaimed enthusiastically.

"It would have been more appropriate for the Muslims to have propagated it before others. The head of state has an assembly of experts in all fields, whose opinion is of assistance to him."

"And is this opinion binding?"

"If there is some difference of opinion they all are retired and elections are held again."

"What an excellent system!" I exclaimed.

"As for agriculture, industry, and trade," continued the sheikh, "they are carried out by those citizens most capable."

"And so it is that there are both rich and poor," I said, remembering some of the scenes I had seen.

"There are also unemployed people, robbers, and murderers," said the sheikh.

"Perfection is with God alone," I said meaningfully with a smile.

"But we have made great headway on that path," he said seriously.

"If only you were to apply the canonical law of Islam!"

"But *you* apply it!"

"The fact is that it is not applied," I insisted.

"Here commitment is to the Authority, applied both in the letter and in the spirit."

"But the state is committed solely to maintaining order and to defense, so it seems to me."

"And public projects which individuals are unable to undertake, such as parks, bridges, and museums. It runs schools which are free to outstanding students who are poor, as well as free hospitals, but most activities are carried on by individuals."

I thought for a while, then asked, "Perhaps you consider yourselves the happiest of people?"

He nodded his head seriously. "It's a relative judgment, Sheikh Qindil, but one cannot generalize with complete confidence so long as there are rich and poor and criminals. Apart from which our life is not devoid of anxiety: there are conflicting interests between us and Haira in

THE JOURNEY OF IBN FATTOUMA

the north and Aman in the south. Thus this unique civilization is threatened and could be wiped out in a single battle; even with victory we could go into a decline if we were to suffer great losses. Also, the religious differences are not always resolved peacefully."

He asked me about my journey and I summarized for him what I had encountered since leaving my homeland. The man was saddened for me and wished me success. "I would advise you," he said, "to hire a sedan chair because the sights of the capital are too numerous for you to see by yourself. We also have many other cities that are worth seeing. As for finding Arousa in our land, it would be easier to reach the land of Gebel."

"I know that perfectly well," I said sorrowfully, "but I have another request: I wish to visit the sage of Halba."

"What do you mean?" he said in astonishment. "Mashriq has its sage and Haira its sage, but here the centers of learning are teeming with sages. With any one of them you will find the knowledge you wish to have, and more."

Thanking him for his conversation and his friendship, I rose to my feet saying, "The time has come for me to go."

"But you will lunch with us at my house," he said, taking hold of me.

I welcomed the invitation as an opportunity to immerse myself in the life of Halba. We walked together for about a quarter of an hour to a quiet street bordered by acacia trees on both sides. We made our way to a handsome building, on the second floor of which lived the imam. I did not doubt that the imam was from the middle class, but the beauty of the reception room gave an indication of the high standard of living in Halba.

I was faced by strange traditions which in my homeland would have been considered inconsistent with Islam, for I was welcomed by both the imam's wife and his daughter, as well as by his two sons. We all sat down at the one table. Even glasses of wine were served. It was a new world and a new Islam. I was disconcerted by the presence of his wife and daughter, for since attaining adolescence I had not shared a dining table with any woman, not even with my own mother. I was uncomfortable and overcome by shyness, and I did not touch the glass of wine.

"Let him do as suits him," the imam said, smiling.

"I see that you follow Abu Hanifa's opinion," I said.

"With us there is no necessity for that," he said, "as individual judgments continue to be made, and we drink according to the weather and traditions, but we do not become drunk."

His wife ran the household, but Samia, his daughter, was a pediatrician at a large hospital, while the two sons were preparing themselves to be teachers. Even more than at the nudity I had encountered in Mashriq, I was amazed at the unrestrained way in which the mother and her daughter took part in the conversation. They talked with a bold and spontaneous frankness just like men. Samia asked me about life in the land of Islam and about the role of women there, and when I had explained the situation she was extremely critical. She made comparisons with women at the time of the Prophet, and the role that they had played then. Then she said, "Islam is wilting away at your hands and you are just standing back and contemplating."

I was also much impressed by her youthful beauty, my admiration the greater for the long time I had been deprived of female company and for my advancing years. The imam related to them something of my life, as well as of my journey and of what I sought to achieve from it.

"He is not, in any event," he said, "one of those who give up."

"You deserve acclaim," said Samia to me.

I was greatly touched by this. Then, in the afternoon, we all performed the prayers behind the imam, and this caused me yet more thoughtful consideration.

The imam's family occupied the depths of my soul even after I had physically left them. On the way back I was overtaken by a yearning for stability and for the warmth of love. Where was Arousa? Where the land of Gebel? Youth had been lost under the ground, so when would I settle down and forge a family and have children? Until when would I remain torn between two conflicting calls?

On the following day I hired a sedan chair, in which I was taken around the important sites of the capital, the centers of teaching, the citadels, the largest factories, the museums, the old quarters. The guide informed me that the people of the different religions acted out the lives of their prophets in the mosques, churches, and temples. I announced my desire to witness the life of our Prophet, may the blessings and peace of God be upon him, so he took me to the biggest of the capital's mosques. I seated myself among the audience and his life was acted out from beginning to end in the courtyard of the mosque. I saw the Prophet, his Companions, and the polytheists: a boldness that approached blasphemy, but I felt I should see everything that deserved to be recorded. The person who performed the role of the Prophet so impressed me that I believed in him, and he affected me more than any vision I had had in my dreams. "What truly astonishes me," I thought, "is that the faith of these people is so sincere and genuine."

I invited the imam and his family to lunch at the inn, thus consolidating my attachment to them still further.

"I shall arrange a meeting for you with a sage of stature named Marham al-Halabi," said the sheikh. I thanked him for his solicitude and we spent a pleasant time together, my heart beating all the while with joy and delight.

On the morning of the following day I left my room at the inn to visit the sage. However, I found many of the guests gathered at the entrance, engaged in animated conversations.

"There is news that one of Haira's leaders has revolted against the king, but that he has failed and has fled to Halba."

"Do you mean that he's now living in Halba?"

"It is said that he is living in one of the oases of Halba."

"The important thing is that the king of Haira is demanding that he be arrested and handed over."

"But that is contrary to the principles of the Authority."

"And his request has been turned down."

"Will the matter end there?"

"There are whispers of war."

"What if the land of Aman seizes the opportunity and attacks Halba?"

"That is the real problem."

Anxiety crept deep into me, feeling I was being chased from one land to another by wars. I wanted to go to the sage but I was frightened when I found the square filled with various demonstrations, meeting up there as though it had been prearranged. I was forced to stay on in the entrance to the inn, looking and listening in a state of extreme astonishment: one demonstration was demanding the handing over of the commander who had fled, another giving dire warning to anyone who handed him over, another demanding that war be declared on Haira, and yet another demanding that peace be maintained at any price. I was overwhelmed by confusion and wondered what a ruler could do faced with such contradictory opinions. I waited until the square had cleared and then hurried to the house of the sage Marham, reaching it an hour late for my appointment. He met me in an elegant room that contained couches and chairs as well as cushions arranged on the floor. I found him to be a tall, thin man in his sixties, with white hair and beard, wrapped round in a lightweight blue cloak. Accepting my apologies for being late, he welcomed me, then inquired, "Would you prefer to sit on chairs or cushions?"

"I like cushions better," I said, smiling.

"That's the way with Arabs: I know you, I visited your countries and studied your cultural background."

"I am not one of the scholars or philosophers of my country," I said shyly, "but I like to acquire knowledge and it is for this that I undertook this journey."

"That alone is sufficient," he said with encouraging quietness. "And what is the goal of your journey?"

I thought for a time, then said, "To visit the land of Gebel."

"I have not known anyone who has visited it or written about it."

"Have you not thought of visiting it one day?"

"He who believes with his mind can dispense with everything."

"The land of Gebel is not my final goal," I added. "I would hope to return from there to my homeland with something that might benefit it."

"I wish you success."

"The fact is that I came here to listen, not to talk," I said apologetically.

"Is there some question that worries you?"

"The life of every people is generally revealed through some basic idea," I said with interest.

Sitting up straight, he said, "Thus lovers of knowledge such as yourself ask us how it is that we have fashioned our life."

"And your life is worthy of provoking such a question."

"The answer is very simple: we have fashioned it ourselves." In concentrated silence I followed what he was saying. "There is no credit for this to any god. Our first thinker believed that the aim of life is freedom, and so from him there issued the first call for freedom, and this has continued generation after generation." He smiled and was silent until his words became firmly embedded in my soul. Then he went on, "Thus I regard everything that liberates as good and everything that fetters as evil. We have set up a system of government that has freed us from despotism. We have dedicated our work to freeing ourselves from poverty. We have achieved outstanding advances in knowledge so that it may free us from ignorance. And so on and so on. It is a long road without an end."

I very carefully committed to memory every word he said.

"The road to freedom was not an easy one," he continued, "and we have paid the price for it in sweat and blood. We were prisoners of superstition and despotism. Pioneers came to the fore, heads fell, revolutions flared, civil wars broke out, until freedom and knowledge triumphed."

I inclined my head in a gesture of admiration for what he was saying. He went on to criticize and make fun of the systems of government in Mashriq and Haira. He also made fun of the system in the land of Aman, which I had not yet visited. Even the land of Islam did not escape censure from his tongue. He must have seen a change on my face, for he grew silent, then said in an apologetic tone, "You are not used to freedom of opinion?"

"Within defined limits," I said gently.

"Excuse me, but one should reconsider everything."

"Your land is not without its poor people and devi-ants," I said defensively.

"Freedom," he said fervently, "is a responsibility which only the competent can be conversant with. Not everyone who belongs to Halba is equal to it. There is no place for the weak amongst us."

"Does not mercy have a value in the same way as freedom?" I inquired hotly.

"This is what the people of the various religions are always saying, and it is they who encourage the weak to remain so. As for me, I find no meaning for such words as mercy or justice—we must first of all agree as to who deserves mercy and who deserves justice."

"I disagree with you completely."

"I know."

"Perhaps you welcome war."

"Yes, if you promise an increase in freedom," he said clearly. "I have not the slightest doubt that a victory by us over Haira and Aman would be the best guarantee for the happiness of their two peoples. Speaking of which, I am for the principle of holy war in Islam."

He went on to give an aggressive interpretation of it, so I applied myself to correcting his theory, but he gave a contemptuous wave of his hand and said, "You have a splendid principle, but you do not possess sufficient cour-age to acknowledge it."

"To what religion do you belong, sage Marham?" I asked him.

"To a religion whose god is reason and whose prophet is freedom," he answered, smiling.

"And all sages are like you?"

"I wish I were able to state that," he said, laughing.

He brought me two books: the first was *The Authority*, or the principal law in Halba, while the second had been written by him and was entitled *Storming the Impossible*. "Read these two books," he said, "and you will know Halba as it really is."

I thanked him for his generosity and for his kind hospitality, then I bade him farewell and left. I had my lunch at the inn, where all tongues were eagerly speaking of the war. In the afternoon I went to the mosque and prayed behind Sheikh Hamada al-Sabki. He then invited me to sit with him and I accepted with pleasure. Then, smiling, he asked me, "Have you found Arousa?"

"Continuing to be attached to Arousa is a meaningless self-delusion," I said seriously.

"That's the truth," he said, confirming my words. Then, after a short silence, he asked, "Will you continue on your journey with the first caravan?"

Feeling slightly embarrassed, I answered, "No, I want to stay on a while longer."

"A good decision. And right in the circumstances, for the king of Haira has prohibited the passage of caravans between Haira and Halba in response to our refusal to hand over the escaped commander."

I was astonished and perturbed.

"The big landowners and the men of industry and business are angry and held an important meeting with the ruler at which they demanded that war be declared," said the sheikh.

"And what is the position of the land of Aman?" I inquired uneasily.

"It's as though you had become an inhabitant of Halba!" said the sheikh, smiling. "The quarrel between Halba and Aman revolves round the ownership of certain wells in the desert between our two lands. The dispute will be settled in favor of Aman right away so that they will not think of treachery."

"I am a stranger," I said uneasily, "and warnings of war are flying all around me."

"The best thing you can do is to remain in Halba. If your stay is extended, you have sufficient funds to allow you to engage in some lucrative business."

I gave up the idea of joining the caravan despite my worry that it could be the last caravan for Aman. I was strongly drawn to Halba by the cleanliness of its atmosphere and by hopes of enjoying myself in the company of some of its inhabitants. I divided my time between sightseeing and the family of Sheikh Hamada al-Sabki. As for Arousa, she hovered as distantly from me as the stars of the night.

Daily life was saturated with thoughts of war. Many were upset at the concessions obtained by Aman without having shed a single drop of blood. The manager of the inn said sullenly, "Despite our sacrifice of the wells, Aman may still double-cross us."

Nerves were strained to the utmost and I was infected by the same feelings as the people around me. I was terrified during the limited hours I spent on my own in the inn, when not sightseeing or with the al-Sabki family. My nerves rebelled and demanded that I find satisfaction in stability. And when Halba declared war and sent its army to Haira my nerves rebelled even more and I began to search around in the violent storm for some safe cave in which to take refuge. People talked of the war, comparing the forces of the two sides and their capabilities, while I strictly confined myself to looking for the means by which to obtain satisfaction in stability. I forgot everything but the objective close at hand, as if I were engaged in a race or being chased. I was encouraged in this by the atmosphere of the family and Samia's sincere friendship, her admiration for me as a traveler, and her sympathy for my never-ending sorrows. "She is a girl of genuine worth," I thought, "and there is no life for me without her."

"I have put my trust in God and have decided to marry," I said to the imam.

"Have you found Arousa?" he inquired.

"Arousa, in any event, is over and done with," I said shyly.

"Have you chosen anyone?"

"What I seek lies with you," I said quietly.

He gave an encouraging smile and asked, "Are you going to marry as someone who is traveling or as someone who stays in one place?"

"I do not think that the dream will vanish," I said truthfully.

"Everything depends upon what she wants. Why don't you yourself speak to her?"

"It is better for you to act on my behalf," I said in embarrassment.

"So be it," he said affectionately. "I appreciate your situation."

I received her agreement the following day. I was impatient to proceed and they complied with my wishes. I rented a flat in the same street and we both furnished it together. The marriage contract was concluded in a quiet atmosphere befitting the circumstances of the war, and so we were brought together in the matrimonial home. My heart was gladdened and I recovered my balance. Encouraging news of the fighting came to us, but sadness forced its way into many hearts, and the prices of innumerable goods rose. Sheikh Hamada al-Sabki suggested I should go into partnership in a shop selling works of art and jewelry, and I agreed with enthusiasm.

My partners were two Christian brothers, and their shop was located in the square where the inn was. The work required me to stay in the shop with them all day long, so—for the first time in my life—I devoted myself to work with commendable zeal. Samia would spend the same hours at the hospital.

"You must make Halba your permanent residence," she said to me. "If you wish, complete your journey, but return here."

"I may think of returning to my homeland," I said frankly, "as I had planned to write my book, but there is nothing wrong in taking up residence here."

"In that event," she said joyfully, "I shall accompany you to your homeland and return with you. As for permanent residence, you will not find such a civilized place as Halba."

I hesitated a while, then said, "It seems to me that my new work will bring us a good income. Wouldn't it be a good idea to think about resigning from your work at the hospital?"

"In our land, work, for man and woman alike, is something sacred," she said with a sweet laugh. "From now on you must think like a man of Halba."

I gazed tenderly at her. "You are all but a mother, Samia."

"That's my affair," she said gaily.

As summer rolled up the last of its pages, the fact that

she was to become a mother became visibly apparent. The breezes of autumn arrived, replete with humidity and the shadows of clouds, and every day I discovered something new from the world of my beloved wife. She had pride without being conceited, she loved to discuss things, she was a true believer, and she was possessed of a strength at which my heart rejoiced.

Perhaps the most extraordinary thing I encountered in my journey was Halba's type of Islam, in which there blazed the contradiction between outward and inward forms. "The difference between our Islam and yours," Samia said to me, "is that ours has not closed the door of independent judgment, and Islam without independent judgment means Islam without reason." What she said reminded me of the lessons of my old master.

However, I was in love with what was feminine in her and with her comeliness, which was so satisfying to my deprived natural impulses. I hungrily pursued that comeliness, heedless of anything else, though her personality was too strong and sincere to be dissolved in the beauty of a ripening woman. I found myself face to face with a brilliant intelligence, an enlightened mind, and exceptional goodness. I was convinced she was superior to me in many things, and this troubled me—I who had not seen woman other than as an object of enjoyment for man. My ardent love for her was commingled with fear and caution. Nevertheless reality demanded that I come to terms with the new situation and meet it halfway, in order to preserve both it and the happiness I had been granted.

"It is a mystery," I said to myself, "that she should give herself to me with such generosity. I am truly fortunate."

Disguising my inner fears, I once said to her, "Samia, you are a priceless treasure."

She told me openly, "And the idea of a traveler who sacrifices security in the cause of truth and goodness intrigues me a great deal, Qindil."

She brought to mind my slumbering project, wakening me from a sleep of honeyed ease, of love, of fatherhood and a civilized life. As though I were spurring on a person anesthetized to reality, I said, "I shall be the first person to write about the land of Gebel."

"Perhaps you will find it more remote than the dream," she said, laughing.

"Then I shall be the first to dispel the dream," I said resolutely.

Autumn passed and winter came in. Its cold was no more severe than that of my homeland, but the rainfall was heavy and one saw the sun but rarely. The winds would blow strongly and noisily, and the thunder would roar loudly and would engrave itself deep within one's soul. People talked of the war, which did not want to come to an end. I shared their feelings with sincerity and wished that freedom might gain the victory over the god-king and that my child might be born in the arms of freedom and security. Then one evening Samia joined me at home after work. She was aglow with a joy that brought to life that bloom of hers undermined by pregnancy. "Rejoice—it's victory!" she exclaimed.

She took off her overcoat, saying, "Haira's army has surrendered, the god-king has committed suicide, and Haira and Mashriq have become an extension of Halba. Freedom and civilization are now destined for their peoples."

Joy entered my heart, though some of the fears engendered by experiences of the past made me inquire, "Will they not pay the price of defeat in some manner?"

"The principles of the Authority are clear," she said enthusiastically. "There is no obstacle in the path of freedom apart from the land of Aman."

"At any event," I said innocently, "it did not double-cross you while you were enduring a long war."

"That's true," she said sharply, "but it is an obstacle in the way of freedom."

The day of the return of the victorious army was a memorable one. All of Halba, men and women, turned out to welcome it and pelt it with flowers, despite the cold weather and the pouring rain. Celebrations of every sort continued for a whole week. I soon noticed, on the way to work, that a strange state of affairs, incompatible with the festivities, was spreading strongly, unhesitatingly. Rumors were flying about as to the number of dead and wounded, rumors that were accompanied by sadness and disquiet. Pamphlets were distributed accusing the state of having sacrificed the sons of the people, not in order to liberate the peoples of Mashriq and Haira, but in the interests of the landowners, industrialists, and merchants; they said that it was a war of convoys of goods, not of principles. Another leaflet I received accused the publishers of the previous ones of being enemies of freedom and the agents of Aman. As a result of this there were noisy demonstrations attacking Aman and challenging the agreement to surrender the water wells. The head of state met with the experts and a unanimous decision was issued nullifying the agreement on the wells and regarding them as jointly owned by Halba and Aman, as they had been before. The people once again began talking about a possible war between Halba and Aman.

Sheikh al-Sabki and his family came to lunch with me, and we sat talking and exchanging views. "If this disturbance," I protested to the sheikh, "is as a result of a decisive victory, what would things be like if it were the result of a defeat?"

"This is the nature of freedom," he said, smiling.

"It reminds me of anarchy," I said frankly.

"It is so for someone who has not had dealings with freedom," he said, laughing.

"I thought you were a happy people," I said bitterly. "But you are torn apart by invisible conflicts."

"The only remedy is yet more freedom."

"And how do you judge, morally, the nullifying of the agreement on the wells?"

"Yesterday I was visiting the sage Marham al-Halabi," he said earnestly, "and he told me that the liberation of human beings is more important than such superficialities."

"Superficialities!" I exclaimed. "One must admit of some moral basis, otherwise the world would be transformed into a jungle."

"But it was and still is a jungle," said Samia with a laugh.

"Look, Qindil," said the imam, "your homeland is the land of Islam, and what do you find there? A tyrannical ruler who rules to please himself, so where is the moral basis? Men of religion who bring religion into subjection to serve the ruler, so where is the moral basis? And a people who think only of the morsel which will fill their stomachs, so where is the moral basis?"

Something seemed to stick in my throat, so I remained silent. Once again I was seized by the memory of my journey. "Will war break out soon?" I asked.

"Only," said Samia, "if one of the two sides feels that it is stronger or if it is overcome by despair."

"Maybe you are thinking of the journey?" inquired my mother-in-law.

"First of all," I answered, smiling, "I must feel assured that Samia is all right."

At the end of winter Samia had her first child, and instead of preparing myself for traveling I gave myself over to the soft life I led between work and home. I immersed myself in the life of Halba, in love, in a high standard of living, in fatherhood, in friendship, and in the treasures of the sky and the parks, which were endlessly beautiful. I dreamt of nothing more delightful than that this state of affairs should continue.

And with the passage of time I became a father to Mustafa, Hamid, and Hisham. However, I refused to admit defeat and would say to myself in shame, "Oh, my homeland! Oh, land of Gebel!"

I was recording some figures in the accounts book at the shop when I found Arousa in front of me. It was no dream, no illusion, but Arousa, dressed in a short skirt and a shawl embellished with pearls, of the sort worn by high-class women in summer. She was no longer young, no longer going about naked, but was still possessed of a decorously dignified beauty. It was as if she were a miracle come out of nowhere. She was turning over in her hands a coral necklace while I looked at her aghast. She happened to turn to me, and her eyes came into contact with my face and grew wider and wider. She forgot herself, and I myself.

"Arousa!" I called out joyfully.

In a daze she answered, "Qindil!"

We stared at each other till we decided, at one and the same time, to recover from our stupor and return to reality. I went to her and we shook hands, oblivious of the astonishment that had overtaken my partner.

"How are you?" I asked her.

"Not bad, everything's fine."

"Are you living here in Halba?"

"Since I left Haira."

"On your own?" I asked after some hesitation.

"I'm married to a Buddhist. And you?"

"Married and a father."

"I didn't have children."

"I hope you are happy."

"My husband is a remarkable and pious man and I have embraced his religion."

"When did you get married?"

"Two years ago."

"I gave up all hope of finding you."

"It's a large city."

"And how was your life before you married?"

She gave a gesture of displeasure. "It was a time of hardship and torture," she said.

"It's unfortunate," I muttered.

"It was for the best," she said, smiling. "We shall journey to Aman, and from there to the land of Gebel, then to India."

"May the blessing of God be with you wherever you may be," I said warmly.

She stretched out her hand and I clasped it, then she took up what she had bought and left. I found myself required to cast some light on the scene which had been enacted in front of my partner. However, I continued my work and kept my emotions to myself, though I knew for certain that everything had come to an end. I told Samia what had occurred, straightforwardly and with apparent indifference. I was not devoid, though, of a feeling of guilt about the excessive interest that flamed in my breast. It was violently shaken and there welled up in it springs of sadness and nostalgic yearnings. Warm gushings from the past flooded over it till it was submerged. While it was not unlikely that the old love had raised its head, had been resuscitated, the new reality was more weighty, more powerful than to succumb to such winds. Nevertheless the hidden desire to undertake the journey awoke in splendor, springing to the fore and searching out the morrow with firm and unrelenting resolve. Fearing that I would rush off to put it into execution, I invented doubts about it and took a decision to postpone it for a year, though during that year I would pave the way by preparing people to accept it.

And so it happened.

My beloved wife gave me permission, neither enthusiastically nor rapidly. I appointed the sheikh to replace me in the business until I should return, and I allocated such dinars for the journey as would give me a good life. I promised that I would return to Halba immediately after the journey and that I would then accompany my wife and children to the land of Islam, where I would compose the book of my journey and find those of my family who were still alive; after this we would return to Halba.

I bade Mustafa, Hamid, and Hisham a heartfelt farewell, as also my wife, Samia, who was bearing within her a new life.

5
The Land of Aman

The caravan moved off, cleaving the dawn darkness, en-
countering the first harbingers of summer. Sheikh al-
Sabki had spoken about the weather of Aman. "Its winter
is killing, its autumn is cruel, its spring is unbearable, so
you can imagine what the summer is like!"

As usual, the caravan reminded me of days past, except
that I had become a mature man affected by destiny. The
light of day shone and revealed a new desert, a desert of
many hills, their sides marked off by low valleys in which
were scattered plants as prickly as hedgehogs, distinguished by their mellow greenness and furious savagery.
After several weeks of travel we reached the area of the
wells, of which there were many. They did not, however,
justify the alarms of war which were threatening the
peace of the two great lands of Halba and Aman. And so
we continued on into country that gradually rose higher,
until we camped on Eagle Hill.

"We shall move off at midnight," said the leader of the
caravan, "in order to arrive by evening at the walls of
Aman."

We continued our journey in pleasant weather until the great wall appeared before us in the light of torches. We came to a stop in front of the gateway. One of the men holding torches came towards us and called out in a rough voice, "Welcome to Aman, the capital of the land of Aman. Welcome to the land of total justice." For a minute the man was silent, then he said, "The merchants will go with a guide to the commercial center, while the travelers will go to the travelers' center."

I did not go to an inn right away as I had done in Mashriq, Haira, and Halba, but followed the guide to a small, solidly built, and clean official house under the charge of armed guards. I was led to a room lit by torches. In the middle sat an official behind a desk, with guards on either side of him, like two statues. I stood before him and he asked me my name and age and how much money I had with me. He also wanted to know about the history of my journey and its purpose. I kept to the absolute truth and the man said, "I shall regard you as a citizen of Halba since you have taken it as a country in which to work and set up a marital home."

I made no objection, and he said, "We shall permit you to stay for ten days, which is sufficient time for a traveler."

"And if I like it here and want to stay on?" I asked.

"In that event submit a request for what you want. We shall then look into it and decide whether to accept it or refuse it." I lowered my head in agreement, concealing my astonishment. "And we shall appoint someone to be your constant companion," he went on.

"Will he be proposed to me so that I can accept or refuse him?" I inquired.

"It is the practice which is followed for the good of strangers." He clapped his hands and there entered the room a short man in his sixties wearing a jacket like a short jubba, a loincloth that reached to the knees, sandals, and a skullcap like a helmet made of cotton or linen.

"Qindil Muhammad al-Innabi," said the official, moving his head from one of us to the other, "Fluka, your guide and representative of the travelers' center."

I left the center with Fluka following me in silence like my shadow, having robbed me of all spirit of adventure and freedom. He lengthened his step and came alongside me and we plunged together into the darkness, finding companionship in the lights from the stars and the flares of the security guards.

"We're on our way to the inn," he said tersely.

By way of a square we approached the inn. It became visible by torchlight and showed up as no less large and luxurious than the one in Halba. As for the room, it was smaller and simpler but lacked none of the amenities. It was also scrupulously clean. I noticed the presence of two beds side by side and asked anxiously, "What's the other bed for?"

"It's for me," said Fluka calmly.

"Are you going to sleep in the same room with me?"
I asked, doing nothing to hide my objection.

"Naturally. What's the point of occupying two rooms
when a single one is sufficient?"

"I would like to be on my own in one room," I said
with displeasure.

"But this is the system followed in our country," he
said, as calmly as before.

"Then I shall enjoy no freedom except in the lavatory,"
I complained.

"And not there either," he said coldly.

"Are you serious?"

"We have no time for idle talk."

I scowled. "It's better to cancel the journey."

"You will not find a caravan for ten days."

He changed his clothes, donning a nightshirt. Making
his way towards his bed, he said, "Everything here is
new and unfamiliar, so free yourself from the fetters of
bad habits."

Faced with reality, I was defeated. I changed my
clothes and went to my bed. For a long time sleep evaded
me because I was so upset, then tiredness overcame me.

With morning I felt uneasy; however, I made as if I
were taking things in my stride. Then Fluka led me to
the dining room, where we sat at a small table and had a
breakfast of milk, pastries, eggs, and crystallized fruit.

Both in quantity and in quality it was excellent; I swallowed it down, all except for a small glass of wine, which I did not touch.

"Wine will be served at every meal," Fluka said. "It's a necessity."

"I have no need of it," I insisted.

"I have known many Muslims who were addicted to it," he said with his habitual calm.

When I smiled and made no comment, he asked, "Do you really believe that your god is concerned whether you drink wine or not?"

When he saw my expression change, he said gently, "My apologies!"

We left the inn together to make our first sightseeing tour. I cast a general look around, then my eyes trembled with something like fear. I was appalled by the empty space. The square and all the streets debouching from it were without trace of any human being. A city empty, deserted, dead. Exceedingly clean and elegant and orderly, with its vast buildings and towering trees, but without any sign of life. I glanced at Fluka in disquiet. "Where are the people?"

"They're at work, men and women," he answered with provocative calm.

"Is there no woman who doesn't work?" I asked him in astonishment. "Isn't there anyone unemployed?"

"Everyone works. There are no unemployed and all women work. As for the old and the children, you will see them in the parks."

"Halba," I answered, unbelieving, "surges with activity, but its streets are always crammed with people."

He thought for some time and then said, "Our system is not similar to any other. Every individual is trained for a job and then works. Every individual gets an appropriate wage. It is the sole land that does not know rich and poor. Here there is a justice that no other land can attain even a measure of."

He pointed at the buildings as we moved from one empty street to another.

"Look, the buildings are all uniform. There are no palaces and no detached houses, no buildings that are vast and others medium-sized. The differences in wages are slight. All are equal other than those whose work sets them aside. The smallest wage is sufficient to satisfy what a respectable person requires in the way of lodging, food, clothing, education, culture, and also entertainment."

I found it hard to believe, and I answered him with platitudes. Nonetheless the sight of the buildings and streets had delighted me, for in their design they were not inferior to those of Halba itself. Fluka took me to a vast park, reached by way of a large bridge over a broad river. I had not seen a park of such size before, nor one with such a variety of trees and flowers. "It's a park for those who have become advanced in years and beyond the stage when they can be active and working," said Fluka. I saw old people of both sexes walking about in the park, taking some gentle exercise, sitting, talking, singing. "In every city there is a similar park."

He said this with pride and satisfaction, and I thought it a good system, the like of which I had not seen in the other lands I had visited. I was struck by the great number of people over eighty years of age. This did not escape the notice of Fluka, who immediately said, "With us, food is characterized by the abundance of basic nutritive ingredients and an avoidance of luxury foods. Also we play sports at certain times during working hours."

One of the curious things I saw in the park was a couple on their honeymoon: a widow and widower in their eighties, they were sitting on the shore of an artificial lake, dangling their feet in its water, which had acquired a green tint from the leaves of the overhanging trees that were mirrored in its surface. I enjoyed watching the people and stayed on in the park for a long time until Fluka said, "The time has come to pay a visit to the children's park."

A spacious square separated it from the old people's park. The square was large enough for a small city to be constructed on it. From a distance, as we approached, came the voices of young children. It was a huge place, like a separate land, crammed with children of all ages.

It possessed numberless playgrounds and areas for study and teaching, with many teachers, male and female.

"Is it for recreation or study?" I asked my companion.

"For both together," he answered. "It is here that we discover different talents, and each is directed in accordance with his inclination and the plan laid down for him. The teachers, men and women, substitute for the fathers and mothers, who are engaged in their work."

"But nothing can replace the tender love of parents," I said innocently.

"Wise sayings and proverbs that no longer have any meaning in the land of Aman," said Fluka quietly.

The morning was not long enough for us to undertake any new visits, so we had our lunch in the inn. It consisted of roast meat and cauliflower, and bread and apples. Before sunset he took me to the big square and we stood under a white poplar tree. "The time has come for you to see the people of Aman."

There were four large streets debouching into the square. With sunset appeared the first signs of human life. It was like the moment of Resurrection. All at once all the streets began to spew forth endless crowds of men and women, each group dressed in the same simple clothes, like an army regiment. Despite the fact that there were successive surging waves of them, they came forward in perfect order, no more than a whisper escaping from them, their faces serious and exhausted, hastening forward, each going to his own goal. One side of the street was given over to those approaching, the other side to those moving away. There was no disturbance, and no merriment either: it was an embodiment of equality, order, and seriousness. It aroused my admiration to the same extent that it stirred within me feelings of anxiety and confusion. The density of the crowd reached its peak, then began gradually to lessen until the empty space won back its total kingdom with the descent of darkness.

"Where have they gone now?" I asked Fluka.

"To their homes."

"Then they return once more to spend their evenings out?"

"No, they stay at home till the morning. As for the places of entertainment, they come alive on the night of the weekend."

"Does this mean that our nights will be spent in the inn?" I asked with concern.

"In the inn for foreigners," he said unconcernedly, "is a place of entertainment where you will find all you want in the way of drink and dancing and singing."

We spent the night there, and though I witnessed a strange form of dancing, a new way of singing, and several games of magic, they were not all that fundamentally different from what I had seen and heard in Halba.

On the following day we visited factories, places of business, and centers for learning and medicine. They were in truth in no way inferior to similar ones in Halba in size, order, or discipline. They all merited my admiration and appreciation and shook my firm belief in the superiority of the land of Islam in matters of civilization and production. However, I did not feel relaxed at the morose expression on the faces of the people, their rigidity, and their overall coldness. It was these traits that had made of my escort, Fluka, a person who, though indispensable, gave me no pleasure.

We visited a revered historic citadel, its walls adorned with inscriptions and pictures. "In this citadel," said Fluka, "there took place the final battle which ended in the defeat of the tyrannical king and the victory of the people."

He took me to a vast building like a temple. "Here you have the court of history. It was here that the enemies of the people were tried and condemned to death."

I asked him whom he meant by the enemies of the people.

"The landowners, factory owners, and despotic rulers. The state gained victory after a long and bitter civil war."

I remembered what my master, Sheikh Maghagha al-Gibeili, had said about not being able to continue his journey because of civil war in Aman. I also remembered the bloody history of Halba in the cause of freedom. And was the history of Islam in our own land any less bloody and full of pain? What does man want? Is it just the one dream? Or are there several dreams according to the number of lands and countries? Is real perfection to be found in the land of Gebel?

"Will you spend tonight in the place of amusement as you did yesterday?" Fluka asked me.

I indicated my lack of enthusiasm through silence.

"Tomorrow the country celebrates Victory Day—it is a memorable event," he said to cheer me up.

We had supper, then sat in the entrance hall of the inn, enjoying the pleasant summer breezes.

"I am a traveler, as you know," I said to Fluka, "and it is the custom in my country for a traveler to record the events of his travels. For this purpose I require much information which the sightseer cannot obtain." He listened quietly, uttering not a word, so I continued, "I would be interested in meeting one of the sages of your land. Can you help me?"

"The sages of the land of Aman," he answered, "are engaged in their duties, but I can provide you with such information as you want."

I quickly swallowed my disappointment and determined to tackle him about the matter. "I want to know about your political system," I said. "How are you ruled?"

"We have an elected president," he replied without hesitation. "He is elected by the small group of the elite who made the revolution—that is, the elite of all the towns, including scholars, sages, and men of industry and agriculture, of war and security. After that he holds the post for life. But if he deviates, they remove him."

That reminded me of the system of the caliphate in the land of Islam, though it also reminded me of the tragic events of our gory history.

"What are his mandatory powers?"

"It is he who is in charge of the army and of security, and of agriculture and industry, of science and art. With us it is the state that owns everything, while the subjects are employees, each working in his own field, there being no difference in this between the sweeper and the president."

"Does no one assist him?"

"His consultants, and the elite group who elected him, but he has the last word. We are thus secured against chaos and indecision."

After some hesitation I said, "But he is too powerful to be made answerable if he deviates."

For the first time he departed from his original emotional coldness.

"The law here is sacred!" he said sharply. Then, before I could say a word, he continued, "Look at nature, its basis is law and order, not freedom."

"But man, unlike other creatures, always strives for freedom."

"It is the voice of carnal greed and illusion. We have found that man's heart is contented only through justice, and so we have made justice the basis of our system, and we have placed freedom under surveillance."

"Is this what your religion orders you to do?"

"We worship the earth, being, as it is, the creator of mankind and the supplier of his needs."

"The earth?"

"It has done nothing for us, but it has created for us the mind, which makes anything else unnecessary."

Then he continued proudly, "Our land is the only one in which you will not come across illusions and superstitions."

Secretly in my heart I asked God's forgiveness for having heard such words. One may find an excuse for the heathenism of the land of Mashriq, likewise that of the land of Haira, but the land of Aman, with its magnificent civilization, how can it worship the earth? It is an extraordinary land. It aroused my admiration to the greatest degree, as well as my disgust. But what saddened me even more was the state to which Islam in my country had sunk, for the caliph is no less despotic than the ruler of Aman. He practices his forms of corruption blatantly, while the religion itself is beset with superstitions and trivialities; as for the people, they are ravaged by ignorance, poverty, and disease. Glorified is He who alone is praised in adversity.

That night I slept in a state of exhaustion and had unpleasant dreams. Then came the day of the feast. As it was a public holiday, the capital took on a look of warmth and liveliness during the whole day. Fluka led me to the palace square. I found that the palace was a lofty citadel, an incomparable architectural masterpiece. In front of it was an immense square, large enough to take thousands upon thousands of people. We took our place in the middle, and the people began arriving and standing in orderly ranks on the perimeter. I looked into their faces with great curiosity. What recurrent pictures they made in their clothes, their faces and bodies! Complexions untouched by a burning sun, bodies strong and slim, faces wreathed in smiles of greeting for the feast, despite their constant scowling aspect on all other days. The beauty of faces in Halba was undoubtedly of a higher order, but the sameness here was itself a matter for astonishment. So it was that one read in people's eyes a certain deep-rooted contentment, also something mysterious that bespoke apathy.

A trumpet was blown to announce the beginning of the festival. From the farthest point of the perimter facing the palace a procession of girls in the bloom of youth came bearing flowers. They walked in four rows towards the palace, then stood in two single files facing each other in front of the great entrance. The groups burst into song, all singing the same anthem, with exciting power and beauty. The sound rose up harmoniously, drawing the groups together into a single ecstatic moment inspired by shared intimate memories. It ended with loud clapping, which went on for two minutes. Fluka nudged me with his elbow and whispered in my ear, "The president is coming."

I looked towards the palace and saw a group of men approaching from shadowy depths. As they drew nearer their features became clearer. The president was walking in front, followed by a group of the ruling elite. He walked on, facing into the perimeter so as to exchange greetings with the crowds nearby. When he passed by me, no more than a few handspans separated him from where I stood. I saw him to be of medium height, excessively fat, and with coarsely distinct features. The members of his retinue were no less fat. This attracted my attention forcibly and I was convinced that the president and his men enjoyed a regime of food which deviated from that to which the people were accustomed. I imagined the sort of conversation that could take place between Fluka and me on that subject. He would tell me that Aman's system was not devoid of privileges reserved to individuals in accordance with their above-average performance in learning or in work, and that it was natural that at the head of such people should be the elected president and his assistants. These privileges were granted within narrow limits that did not permit the existence of any class distinctions and, for understandable reasons, had no connection with the privileges of families, tribes, and classes in other societies ruled by injustice and corruption. The fact is that I did not find in that anything to contravene the just code in force in the land of Aman, and I did not find in it any point of resemblance with what occurs in other countries, the land of Islam at their head, in the form of shocking disparity in the way people are treated. It occurred to me that I was seeing things more clearly than previously. Yes, the land of Halba has a target that it has painstakingly realized, and the land of Aman too has a target that it has painstakingly realized. As for the land of Islam, they announce a target and achieve a different one, thoughtlessly, shamelessly, and without reckoning. Is perfection really to be found in the land of Gebel?

The president returned and ascended to the dais in front of the palace. He began addressing his people, expounding to them the history of their revolution, their victory battle, and what had been achieved for them in the different spheres of their life. I concentrated on following the emotions exchanged between the man and the people, and I did not doubt their enthusiasm and the way in which they shared single hopes and a similar vision. They were not a nation that was downtrodden and helpless, nor one that had lost its consciousness and breeding. Perhaps it lacked something important, perhaps its happiness was flawed; nevertheless I saw it as a cohesive nation with a message that was not without a faith of some sort.

When the president finished his speech a troop of cavalry forged its way into the square. On the tips of their lances were human heads. My heart turned over at the awfulness of the sight. I looked towards Fluka and he said brusquely, "Rebellious traitors!" There was no time to discuss the matter. The people again sang the anthem and the festival ended with general cheering.

We returned to the inn to have our lunch. During lunch Fluka said, "Did the sight of the severed heads upset you? It was necessary, inevitable. Our system demands that no one should interfere in what does not concern him and that each individual should concentrate on his own affairs. Thus the engineer should not chatter about medicine, the worker shouldn't become absorbed in the affairs of the peasant, and internal and external politics are no business of anyone's. He who rebels against this is punished in the way you saw."

I realized that personal freedom had execution for its punishment in this land, and this caused me great sadness. I felt exasperated at Fluka for his fanatical belief in what he said.

We spent our evening at a large circus which was crammed with people, and we watched all sorts of games, singing, and dancing, which were pleasantly amusing. Then we dined off roast meat and fruits. Fluka drank and invited me to join him, and when I did not do so he was forced to moderate his drinking, which put him in a bad temper. We left the circus at midnight and walked slowly under the moonlight in streets filled with reeling drunkards.

"How pleasantly you amuse yourself!" I said, wishing to make conversation.

"And how pleasant is your seriousness!" he said, smiling for the first time, either because of the festival or because of the wine he had drunk.

He saw me smile and was not happy at my smile. "Do you find life in your first homeland or your second homeland better than life in Aman?"

"Let's not talk about my first homeland, for its people have betrayed their religion," I said bitterly.

"If the system does not provide the means by which its application is guaranteed, then it won't survive," he said roughly.

"We haven't yet lost hope."

"Then what's the point of going to the land of Gebel?"

"Knowledge is light," I said listlessly.

"It is nothing more than a journey to nothingness," he sneered.

The days followed one another tediously, and the people at the inn began talking about relations between Halba and Aman in tones of pessimism and apprehension. I asked Fluka what lay behind this. "In their war with Haira they pretended to recognize our right to the wells, and when they were victorious they withdrew their recognition with utterly despicable baseness. Today it is said that they are mobilizing an army from the two countries which they have occupied, Mashriq and Haira, and this means war."

I was overwhelmed by disquiet. "And will war really break out?"

"We are totally prepared," he answered coldly.

My thoughts hovered round Samia and the children. I remembered the tragedy of Arousa and her children. I anxiously awaited the expiry of ten days. One day and then another passed without incident. My heart calmed down and I began to prepare for the journey. During that time it occurred to me to ask Fluka about the Buddhist traveler and his wife, Arousa, who had visited Aman a year ago, and he affirmed that he would be able to provide me with information about them when we went to the travelers' center at the end of my stay. The man kept his promise and himself consulted the files. "The couple stayed ten days in the land of Aman, then went off in a caravan bound for the land of Ghuroub. However, the husband died on the way and was buried in the desert. As for the wife, she continued her journey to the land of Ghuroub."

The news shook me. I wondered where Arousa could be and how she was, and would I find her in the land of Ghuroub or had she gone to the land of Gebel—or returned to Mashriq?

At dawn I was at the stopping place of the caravan with my luggage. I shook Fluka by the hand. "Thank you for your good companionship and the benefits you conferred on me."

He pressed my hand in silence, then whispered in my ear, "War has broken out between Halba and Aman."

I was so upset that I could not continue our talk; I did not even ask who had started the war.

Memories of Samia and the children—and even the child about to be born—dominated me.

6

The Land of Ghuroub

The caravan plunged into the darkness of the dawn, while I looked round at everything with a heart filled with anxiety. Never had it been vouchsafed to me to travel with a heart composed and a soul untroubled; always apprehensions enveloped me. My fevered imagination hovered round Halba, praying that Samia, Mustafa, Hamid, and Hisham be kept safe, wondering in perplexity about the result of that bloody struggle between the two most powerful lands. I raised my eyes to the flowering garden of the sky and muttered, "Be with us, O God of the heavens and the earth." The earth gave out its Lord's light and I saw a vast level desert under gentle summer weather; I also saw gazelles leaping about here and there, so that I called it "the desert of gazelles."

The journey extended for a month and we were not greatly discomforted, which made us think that it would have a good outcome. Towards the end of one night a voice gave us the good news that we had reached the boundaries of the land of Ghuroub. It was a half-moon and the weather was silvery, but I saw neither a city wall nor a customs agent.

"This is a land without guards, so enter it in safety and peace," said the owner of the caravan, laughing.

"How shall I know the way to the inn of the foreigners?" I asked him.

"The light of day will indicate to you what you are looking for," he said, continuing to laugh.

I stayed full of curiosity till the sun came up. Perhaps it was the most beautiful sun I had known in my life, for it gave off a light that held no troublesome heat, a light that was accompanied by a gentle breeze and a pleasant fragrance. In front of me there stretched out a limitless forest. My gaze did not fall on a single building, a single hut, house, or palace. Nor did I see a soul. It was a new riddle for me to puzzle out—but what should I do with my baggage? I returned to the owner of the caravan and he said, "Leave it where it is and don't be afraid—go off in peace and return in peace."

I chose a spot close by a well, which I took for a landmark. I put down the cases and lodged my money in a belt which I wore round my waist under my robe. I then went off on an exploratory tour. I walked on luxuriant grassy ground that had been planted with date palms and fruit trees, between which were located springs of water and small ponds. At first the land appeared to be devoid of human beings, until I saw the first person, who was sitting squat-legged under a date palm. He was an elderly man with white hair and a long beard; he was silent and was either dozing or in a trance, a recluse with no companion, male or female. I approached him as though I had come across some treasure.

"Peace be upon you, brother," I said to him.

As it did not appear that he had heard me, I repeated my salutation, saying, "I am a traveler and am in need of a word to show me the way."

Not a sound came from him and he remained lost in his own realm.

"Do you not wish to talk to me?" I asked him.

He showed no reaction. It was as if I had no existence, so I gave up hope of him. Reluctantly, I turned and continued on my way. As I pressed on further I came across other people in the same state, both men and women, and I would again make the effort and would be refused or ignored until it seemed to me that it was a forest full of deaf, dumb, and blind people. I cast a general enraptured look at the beauty all around me and muttered to myself, "It's a paradise without people." I took some of the fruit that had fallen to the ground and ate till I was satisfied, then returned to where my baggage was and saw that the traders were filling their sacks with fruit, as much as they wanted. When the owner of the caravan saw me he laughed. "Were you able to engage any of them in conversation?" I shook my head, and he said,

"It's a paradise of people in a trance, but its bounties are spread about in great abundance."

"What do you know of them?" I asked him eagerly.

"There's an old man in the forest," he said indifferently, "who is much sought after. Maybe he will provide you with what you are seeking."

A traveler's hope was brought to life anew and I was intoxicated with the joy of victory.

"How beautiful the summer is here!" I said.

"All the seasons are like this," replied the man.

I rose with the sun, invigorated and optimistic. I heard one of the traders say, "We shall go on coming and going between Aman and Ghuroub till the war ends and the roads are again open to caravans."

I made off into the depths of the forest, proceeding for hours at a time without stopping until I heard from afar the sounds of communal singing. I went towards the sound and saw a group of men and women sitting on the ground in the form of a crescent in front of an old man seated under a luxuriant tree. It was as if he were teaching them how to sing and they were repeating the sounds after him with the utmost tenderness. I drew near and crouched behind them. I looked at the man and saw that he was elderly and naked except for a loincloth. A halo of light seemed to encircle his pure face and magnetic eyes. He brought the singing, or the lesson, to a close, and the men and women rose and dispersed quietly.

Arousa was not among the women. I had not come across her on the previous day, but the perfume of her was diffused in the atmosphere with the aroma of fruit and green grasses. There was no one in the place except the old man and me. I stood humbly before him and he looked at me with his limpid eyes and I felt that I existed. The sense of estrangement that had been choking me yesterday in the forest had vanished and I now belonged to the land of Ghuroub. The journey had not been undertaken in vain. I raised the palms of my hands to my forehead in greeting and said, "Master, you are my long-awaited goal."

"A newcomer?" he asked, scrutinizing my face.

"Yes."

"What do you want?"

"I am a traveler who goes from land to land in search of knowledge."

He closed his eyes for a mintue, then opened them. "You left your land for knowledge and yet you have turned aside from the target many times and have wasted valuable time in darkness. Your heart is divided between a woman you have left behind you and a woman you are striving to find."

I was truly amazed and looked at him in awe.

"How is it you have the ability to read what is hidden?"

"Here they do that—and more," he said simply.

"Are you the ruler of this land?"

"There is no ruler of this land. I am the instructor of those who are perplexed."

"Increase me in understanding!" I said earnestly.

"Everything is pledged for its due time."

I pointed to those around me. "Why do people not say a greeting or listen to what one says?"

"Their life here is conformity with truth and withdrawal from humankind."

"They look as if they are in a trance."

"Patience in the face of the bitterness of misfortune is the door to the sweetness of intimate discourse."

I gave thought to what I had just heard, then I asked, "And what is their goal in all this?"

"They are all emigrants. They come from all different parts to avoid depraved desires and to prepare themselves for the journey to the land of Gebel."

I was moved by mention of the name and said joyfully, "Then I shall find companions in my final journey."

A smile showed up in his eyes. "Like them," he said, "you must prepare yourself."

"How much time does it take?"

"Each one according to his ability. One's zeal may slacken, and then one will be advised to remain on in Ghuroub."

I was disheartened. "And if one insists on going?"

"There is the fear that he will be treated over there like a dumb animal."

"And how do you prepare them for the journey?" I inquired, extremely perplexed.

"Everything depends on them," he said clearly. "I train them with singing to prepare the way, but they themselves must extract the powers hidden within themselves."

"I have never heard such things before," I said, puzzled.

"This is the case with every newcomer."

"What does it mean," I asked humbly, "to extract from within myself hidden powers?"

"It means that in every person are treasures that have been covered over and which he must search out—especially if he wants to visit the land of Gebel."

"And what is the connection between this and the land of Gebel?"

He was silent for a time, then said, "Over there they rely in their life on these treasures and don't use senses or limbs."

"Won't you give me an idea about these treasures?" I said urgently.

"Don't be in a hurry."

"And when will I know that I have been successful?"

"When you are able to fly without wings," he said calmly.

I regarded him closely in stupefaction. Then, affected by his seriousness and sincerity, I said, "Perhaps you are speaking to me in metaphors."

"No, it's the plain truth. The land over there is based on these forces and through them has come near to attaining perfection."

"You will find me to be sincere," I said with determination.

"Your reward will be to dwell in the land of Gebel."

"It will be only a visit, after which I shall return to my country," I said hastily.

"Through it you will forget the world and all that's in it," he said with conviction.

"But my motherland is in need of me."

"And how did you leave it?" he asked in amazement.

"I undertook the journey in the hope of returning to it with experience which would provide it with its salvation."

"You are a deserter," the old man said with displeasure. "You made your journey a pretext for fleeing from your duty. No one has emigrated here except after discharging his duty. Some have lost the bloom of youth in prison for the sake of holy war, not by reason of a woman."

"I was a lone individual in the face of total tyranny," I exclaimed in anguish.

"That's the excuse of a man weak in spirit."

"Let the past be as it may, my determination will not be impeded and my life will not be squandered uselessly."

He took refuge in silence. Regarding this silence as

assent, I took courage and said, "You will find me a man of determination and sincerity."

I stood up, bowing my head humbly. A thought occurred to me, but I hesitated, alarmed at making it known, when he said, "Do you want to know what time has done to Arousa?"

I was as astonished as when he had seized my past from the shadows. I asked myself: Is this how they make themselves understood in the land of Gebel?

"She has gone already to the land of Gebel," he said.

"Has she been successful in embarking upon the experience?" I asked in surprise.

"By virtue of the pains she suffered in her life," he said, smiling.

When I was about to depart he inquired, "What is the use of dinars hoarded around your waist?" I returned to the caravan's stopping place and put the dinars in one of my bags.

"We are leaving at dawn tomorrow," said the owner of the caravan.

"I am remaining," I said casually.

Immediately after dawn I was the first to make my way to the gathering of my master. I was joined by a group of newcomers and we sat in a crescent, naked except for something to cover our loins.

"Love work," said the old man, "and do not pay attention to the fruits and the reward." He was silent for a while and then continued, "The first step on the ladder is the ability to concentrate fully." He clapped his hands together and said, "By full concentration man merges into his essence."

He began singing while we sang in time with him. The singing raised me to another world. At each musical phrase there gushed forth a source of power from my inner consciousness.

I returned to my place under a date palm and started to practice. I struggled with concentration and it struggled with me. I joined in a heated battle with the pictures of my past life. They would assault me with love and fidelity and I would chase them off with the bitterness of distress, and the days would pass filled with torture, resolution, and hope. At the beginning of each lesson, before the singing and the chanting, he would counsel us to love work and to ignore the fruits and the reward.

"Thus is affection cemented between you and the soul of existence," he would say. He would also counsel us to concentrate, saying, "It is the opener of doors to hidden treasures."

"Over there, in the land of Gebel," he would say with conviction, "with mind and hidden powers they discover truths, till the land, construct factories, and bring about justice, liberty, and universal purity."

I returned to my solitude, imagining the day when I would employ my hidden powers against everything that is crooked and twisted in my homeland so that I might set it anew in an upright manner for an upright people. The days passed and I forgot time and did not know how many days and months had gone by. My cup was filled with confidence, and in its darknesses there glittered flickerings of inspiration.

One day I awoke before dawn, earlier than my usual time. I went at once to the old man and found him sitting under the light of the stars. I took my seat, saying, "Here I am, Master."

"What has brought you?" he asked me.

"A call that emanated from you," I said firmly.

"This is a first step to success," he said contentedly. "A downpour of rain starts with a few drops."

We remained silent as we waited for the arrival of the groups of people until our crescent was complete. The face of the old man in the light of the rising sun was despondent. He began singing as usual and we intoned after him, but we were not intoxicated with joy. Before we left he said to us, "Evil is coming, so meet it with the courage that is worthy of you." He added not a word to that, ignoring our questioning eyes.

In the early morning of the following day we awoke to uproar and the neighing of horses. On looking up we saw torches spread out above the earth like stars: an army of horsemen and foot soldiers had without warning thrown a cordon around Ghuroub. Everyone hurried off to where the old man was and sat around him in calm silence. Then they began to sing until the sun came up, at which a commander followed by guards made his appearance in front of us. From the first glance I knew that they were from the army of Aman, and I wondered anxiously whether they had conquered Halba.

"Owing to the war which is going on between us and Halba," said the commander, "and because we have heard that Halba is thinking of occupying Ghuroub in order to encircle Aman, considerations of safety demand that we occupy your land." Silence reigned and no one from our side commented with so much as a word. The commander went on, "If you want to remain, you must plant the land and join those people who are working. If not, we shall make ready a caravan that will take you to the land of Gebel."

Once again silence reigned. It was broken by the old man addressing his words to us. "Choose for yourselves what you want."

Several voices called out, "The land of Gebel . . . the land of Gebel . . ."

"You will encounter hardship because of your lack of training," warned the old man.

Insistently they called out, "The land of Gebel . . . the land of Gebel . . ."

"Whoever is found here after the caravan moves off," said the commander firmly, "will be regarded as a prisoner of war."

7
The Beginning

At dawn the caravan left the land of Ghuroub. For the first time it was made up wholly of travelers and emigrants: not a single merchant was to be found in it. We were enfolded in anxiety, sadness, and apprehension because of what had occurred in the land of Ghuroub, where we had been forcibly cut off from our training. I wished that on the way opportunities might be afforded us for resuming meditation and exertion in order to lessen the hardship that awaited us.

The rising of the sun revealed a flat desert throughout which were scattered many wells. For a month we continued until our way was barred by the Green Mountain, stretching in both directions as far as the eye could see. We had to cross the mountain, ascending it, then going down the other side. In front of us lay a wide pathway that rose gently upwards, so the caravan headed towards it. At infrequent intervals there were bouts of light rain which kept us company in our loneliness. We would travel by day and encamp at night. Then, after three weeks, we reached the highest part of the mountain. It was a broad, flat area rich with vegetation. "There is the land of Gebel for you," said the old man, standing at the edge and pointing.

He was indicating another mountain separated from the Green Mountain by a desert. On the top of it stood the city, tall and extensive, with vast domes and buildings bespeaking sublime majesty. I looked in its direction with stunned fascination. It was no longer a dream but a reality, a reality that was close at hand, for there was nothing between us and it except for us to descend the mountainside, cross the short space of desert, and ascend the other mountain. We would then find ourselves in front of the city entrance, with its director of customs saying to us, "Welcome to the land of Gebel, the land of perfection."

Our patience had diminished and we hastened to be on our way. It took the caravan two weeks to descend the side of the mountain and reach the desert. I was taken aback when I saw the desert stretching away as though endlessly in front of us. We could hardly see the other mountain, so immersed was it in the distance. Astonished at how our eyes had deceived us, I was sure that many days and weeks would pass before we reached the other mountain, on the top of which was to be found the land of Gebel. And we did in fact journey for many weeks, the distance increased by the hills and elevations that barred our way, forcing us to turn sometimes to the right, sometimes to the left, until it seemed to me that a whole lifetime had gone by before we reached the base of the other mountain. We stood below it looking upwards and found that it was as high as the clouds themselves, defying our longings. Then the master of the caravan said, "Here is where the caravan ends, gentlemen."

I could not believe my ears.

"But take us up," I said, "to the land of Gebel."

"The mountain pass is narrow, as you can see," replied the man, "and gives no room for a camel."

We hurried off to our spiritual master and he said gently, "The man is speaking the truth."

"And how shall we continue our journey?"

"On foot, as those before us have done," he said casually.

"For those who find the going too difficult, let them return with the caravan," said the master of the caravan.

But nobody's determination weakened and we all decided to venture forward. I thought about myself and those I had left behind, and about the circumstances I would meet that might prevent my returning. With all this in mind, it occurred to me to write out a journal of my travels and to give it to the master of the caravan to hand over to my mother or to the custodian of the House of Wisdom, for there are aspects that deserve to be known. There are even references to the land of Gebel itself which will disperse some of the darkness that has settled over it and will stir the imagination to picture things about it that are not yet known. After this it would be no bad idea to set aside a special journal for the land of Gebel, should I be destined to visit it and return to my homeland.

The man agreed to undertake the task, so I made him a present of a hundred dinars and we recited together the opening chapter of the Quran to seal the agreement. After that, freeing myself of my misgivings, I made ready for the final adventure with unabated determination.

With these words ends the manuscript of the voyage of Qindil Muhammad al-Innabi, known as Ibn Fattouma.

No history book makes any mention further of this traveler.

Did he complete his journey or did he perish on the way?

Did he enter the land of Gebel? How did he fare there?

Did he stay there till the end of his life, or did he return to his homeland as he intended?

Will one day a further manuscript be found describing his last journey?

Knowledge of all this lies with the Knower of what is unseen and of what is seen.

About the Author

Certainly the most world-renowned of Arabic novelists, NAGUIB MAHFOUZ was born in Cairo in 1911 and began writing when he was seventeen. A student of philosophy and an avid reader, he has been influenced by many Western writers, he says, including Flaubert, Zola, Camus, Dostoevsky, and, above all, Proust. Awarded the Nobel Prize for Literature in 1988, Mahfouz has more than thirty novels to his credit, among them his masterwork, *The Cairo Trilogy*. He lives in the Cairo suburb of Agouza with his wife and two daughters.

About the Translator

Born in Vancouver, DENYS JOHNSON-DAVIES began studying Arabic at the School of Oriental Studies, London University, and later took a degree at Cambridge. He has been described by Edward Said as "the leading Arabic-English translator of our time," and has published nearly twenty volumes of short stories, novels, and poetry translated from modern Arabic literature. He lives much of the time in Cairo.